WHEN THE COLOR STARTED: STORIES

BRADFORD PHILEN

TAILWINDS PRESS

Copyright © 2020 by Bradford Philen. All rights reserved. Except as permitted under the U.S. Copyright Act of 1976, no part of this publication may be reproduced, distributed, or transmitted in any form or by any means, or stored in a database or retrieval system, without the written permission of the publisher.

Tailwinds Press
P.O. Box 2283, Radio City Station
New York, NY 10101-2283
www.tailwindspress.com

Published in the United States of America
ISBN: 978-1-7356016-0-1
1st ed. 2020

CONTENTS

WHEN
THE COLOR
STARTED

"FIGHT NIGHT"

Cleveland woke to roosters crowing at daybreak down-stairs in one of the hotel garden courtyards. He and Anong had left the balcony door open by accident the night before, enjoying the cool beach breeze, drinking Chang beer and swigging *sang som* whiskey, fucking and falling asleep to a Steven Seagal movie marathon playing on one of the cable television channels. Now, a slight hangover, his head felt heavy. He looked at the flat, ruffled sheets next to him. Anong had already gone, but he could still smell her moist, tamarind skin and the bergamot lotion from Victoria's Secret she kept at the bedside. The stifling summer Thai air tasted like a spiced mango lodged in his throat. He chugged water, put on his swim trunks and running shoes, and left.

Jogging was one of his daily routines, even on a fight night. The hotel staff saw Cleveland and nodded excitedly, too spry and cheery, as usual. I am a spectacle, Cleveland thought, but he figured he'd been there long enough to not get the *why you running* smile and stare. Ten years in Asia, the last four of those in Phuket. He sprinted through the hotel parking lot until he reached a cobblestone path lined with palm trees by the beach. He slowed to a jog—partly because he thought he might vomit.

He watched soft waves break on the shore. The town felt tired, but in Phuket time didn't matter. It was either day or night. The day was recovery: motorized street sweepers spewed sanitizers that swabbed the filth and then sank into sewers and drains that eventually led to the Andaman Sea. The night was neon: blinking, flashing, pulsing, pumping, jerking the rhythms of passersby, the naughty night-crawlers.

Early sunbathers had set out on the beach already, mostly too-tanned Europeans or Russians obsessed with the sun. On the town side of the street, security grilles closed the shops and market entrances; only a 7-Eleven and a coffee shop were open. He ran well past the main business district and ascended Thaweewong road. The morning sky was more clear and crisp than the rest of the day; a strange haze would settle by noon because of burning forests and the burning flesh of wild monkey corpses somewhere in Indonesia.

At the top of Thaweewong road he stopped and gazed at the beach below. His chest heaved. He thought about Anong and how he loved her and how beautiful it was or would become. And then just like that, as effortless as the breeze, he had another thought and his mood changed. Why had she left that morning? She usually waited for him to return from his run or she'd wake with him so they could have breakfast together. But not today.

He realized he had sweated out his headache, but could still go faster. There were more beach-goers below him now and they looked like ants, he thought, which was a cliché, but that's all he could think of. Ants scurrying along sandy borderlines until they stepped into the water and it swallowed them and they looked like ants either floating or drowning. Ants either float or drown.

Boredom scared Cleveland. He ran faster along Thaweewong road, which continued up and down jungle hillsides and patches of lemongrass and murky-greenish ponds of water lilies and torn plastic bags strewn along sagging branches of forgotten flora and stretches of palm and coconut forests and banana trees and clouds of humid air thicker than paint and finally he arrived at a village he'd reached before, he was sure. Debris and garbage littered the dusty road and stray dogs wandered like boys on summer break, thinking themselves invincible. Smoke curled from burning wood stoves; villagers sat and stood and drove motorbikes and three-wheeled tuk-tuks.

He stopped by a roadside vendor's shop and asked for water. The vendor, a woman of an indeterminate age, smiled and waved her hand at him in a movement that looked like a butterfly flapping through the air.

"I know you. I know you," she said and disappeared quickly to the back of the shack.

Cleveland knew the feminine Thai-English accent well—it carried syllables a little longer and higher at the end of each sentence, phrase, or word even. His heart beat fast. He was tired. The woman returned with a stack of poster flyers for Muay Thai fighting events. She scanned and flipped through them with the quickness and precision of a librarian.

"Yes-yes," she said, wiping dust from one of the laminated posters and then shaking her head *yes*. "You, no? Ah-ha, you see, I know you."

That *is* me, Cleveland thought. Fists raised, elbows wide, face stern, eyes staring with an empty, almost aloof gaze: picture worse than any mug-shot he'd ever had. He tried to remember that fight, but couldn't recall . . . the fights. How many had there been? *Oh-Ya-Yo!* He hadn't come up with that. He'd told the ring officials his name was Cleveland, and they said, "like Ohio?" Ohio *was* easier, and then he pummeled the local champion El Papi in three rounds. It was a knockout. *Who can beat Ohio?* the crowd yelled, but it sounded like *Oh-ya-yo. No one can beat Oh-ya-yo, he's too fast and too strong. Too fast, too strong. Too . . .* You are a fighter, Cleveland. Always. You are the Miracle Baby, remember.

"For you," the woman said, "beer free."

"I need water," Cleveland said. He took two slimy

twenty baht bills from his sweaty shorts pocket.

"Oh," she said. "Water sixty-five baht, not forty. Sorry. Just for you, beer free."

He paid the woman and as he exited he thought he spotted Anong climbing onto the back of a motorbike. But it can't be Anong, he thought. He looked closer, examining the girl's thin waist and firm, stout legs. Anong was the shortest girl he'd ever been with. Same perky breasts. The girl's long, russet hair hid her face. Cleveland nearly dropped the open water bottle in his hand.

"Anong," he said, calling to her.

She didn't hear him, and the driver, a young Thai man, made a U-turn on the road. As they passed the vendor's shop, Cleveland stepped out in front of the motorbike. It was an impulsive step that Cleveland wasn't even sure why he made. He saw the driver's eyes full of panic and confusion. He looked again at the girl; it wasn't Anong. The motorbike swerved past him and almost skid off the road. Neither the driver nor the girl wore a helmet. The man stopped the motorbike, turned, and stared at Cleveland. The girl jabbed a pointing finger and yelled. Cleveland didn't know what to do so he pressed his palms together and bowed, something he did before and after a fight, and while he knew it was a shameful attempt at an apology, he knew he would get away with it because of his boring Aryan skin and beach-blue eyes. He didn't have to remember that; it was innate.

He watched the girl on the motorbike turn to the man and hold him tightly from where she sat behind him on the saddle. The man kicked-started the motorbike again and revved the engine. They drove away. Cleveland guzzled the rest of his water and ran in the direction he'd come from.

At quarter to two Cleveland heard a knock on his hotel room door and thought it was a cleaner or an employee to refill the refrigerator bar. He'd moved from place to place, hotel to hotel, since he'd been in Phuket, but settled at Bhukitta Village Palace seven months ago; it was no palace, but it was on the beach, affordable, and offered free breakfast, in-room WiFi, and discounted rates for long-term stays. He had been resting in bed, falling in and out of sleep, surfing cable channels. "No," he said. "I don't need anything now. Thank you."

"Oh-ya-yo," a voice said.

It was Anong. He stirred from the bed and tied his robe.

"Knock, knock, Oh-ya-yo. This no clean lady."

The room was cooler than she liked so he turned off the air conditioner and then opened the door. He leaned in the doorway. "Hi," he said.

Anong smiled. She was dressed in the same clothes from the night before—short-short jean shorts inconspicuously torn and fringed on purpose, scarlet red tank top and matching heels, not too high. She'd slung the purse he had bought her over her shoulder: smooth, red, snakeskin leather, gold buckle, thick brown leather strap. She'd picked it out. She reached her hand to his neck and he bent toward her. They kissed.

Cleveland felt a heavy rush of something warm and flooding cover him then. Something magical and invincible. She withdrew first. He found her eyes and remembered waking alone and then paranoia pricked him again. Something like despair tickled his throat. "Where did you go this morning?"

She sighed and reached to kiss him again. Their teeth clinked. He looked at her, and there was a pause, and he knew what could happen: he could take her right then and there however he wanted, over and over and over and over—to the point of his own, sad exhaustion, like a hamster tiring himself at his cage wheel. They were good at sex. But for Cleveland, there were rituals: no sex before a fight.

"Oh-ya-yo," she said softly. "No worry me. I here with you now-now."

Was that a begging whisper, he thought. A riveting Thai beauty, standing here at the door. Did rules and rituals really matter? He couldn't help himself. Swiveling insides. He pulled her toward him.

"Oh," she said.

He started to untie his robe, but she held him still then.

"Ah, ah, ah," she said. She allowed one more kiss and then held him back. "No funny-funny before fighting." She kidded him, mocked his Muay Thai moves, jabbed his chest and stomach. He loved it. "Unless you *want* it now-now," she said.

Outside on the beach, swimmers and sunbathers rode jet skis through the bay and out into the ocean and surfers and waders and beach walkers were clad in next-to-nothing and vendors sold Chang beer right on the beach and it was midday, the time to soak in the sun and wait for the night.

Cleveland looked at Anong again. Soft skin. Subtle freckle on her lip. Silky hair strewn perfectly so it cuddled her face and neck, then tickled and paved her shoulders. "Why do you torture me?" he said.

"Maybe you love me too much."

Love her, he thought. Yes. I do, don't I? Why can't I? You are a fighter. You are a miracle, remember. Fight, and she will love you. She has to. "Where'd you go today?" he said.

"To see my friend Kanda. She sick, so I take look her. She live near airport, too far-la, so I go early."

He hadn't met Kanda before, but he'd heard Anong talk about her often. They had "worked" together. Anong said she knew Kanda was a real, true friend because they always laughed at the same time.

Cleveland actually knew little about Anong—in regard

to her life, where she came from. She said Udon Thani, and Cleveland knew that was in the north, where many of the hot, young things came from. But what was life like there? She said her father farmed rubber and rice. Cleveland said he didn't know you could farm rubber. *My mother Vietnamese*, she'd told him. *I have six sisters.* He didn't ask too many questions. That world—rubber farming in the north—seemed like another galaxy away.

Cleveland knew what "work" meant for Anong. That was before, wasn't it? Before me, he thought. It was an umbrella title for the things she did when men hired her to do *fun things* and *naughty-naughty stuff*: tour guide, masseuse, escort. There was more. It was a livelihood. "Is Kanda very sick? Does she need money?"

"No," she said. "I just visit her because I love her." She pulled the purse from one shoulder and settled it on the other. "I see you later tonight. Okay-la?"

"Why did you come here now?"

"To tell you have good fight."

"You mean to wish me luck."

"No luck. Have good fight." She looked at him. "Remember, I thinking you."

He thought about breaking his no-sex-before-a-fight rule. He pulled her toward him and wanted to say, *don't leave me.* They kissed again, and she told him again to have a good fight and began to back away. He blew her a kiss, and then, as he was closing the door, she said, "Wait."

"Yes?"

"You want me next month like this month?"

He looked at her, envisioning himself saying a million other things, but settled on: "That would be nice. Same, yes, next month." Their arrangement was 15,000 THB per month. He sponsored Anong, which meant he paid for her time so that she only "worked" for him.

"Maybe," she said then, "you can pay me early? I need send money home, Songran is coming soon-soon."

"Sure," he said. "How's tonight, after the fight?"

She smiled *yes*. "Message me when you want me, okay-la?"

For now, he kept the engagement ring in a tiny laced sack that wasn't big enough to hold two nickels stuffed in his gym bag. At one-and-a-half carats, he'd bought it from a Nigerian man named Bobo who owned a jewelry shop at Jungceylon, the newest mall by the Patong beach area, and said he had the best real diamonds in all of South East Asia.

Cleveland had a few more hours before he had to leave for Patong Stadium. Flipping channels again, he found the next Seagal movie: *Above the Law*. It was near the end. There was a fight scene and Seagal killed all the enemies with swanky martial arts moves and clever makeshift weaponry.

He fell asleep and found himself in a rowboat paddling through a thick, cream colored sea. It parted like gravy, and he didn't want to touch the surface or think what might be beneath it. Restless, he looked behind him: nothing. Above him: an endless pastel blue sky soared. Finally, in front of him: another boat. He paddled faster. He thought it was Anong. Her face wasn't clear, but it was her body. Her legs. Shoulders. Petite, perky tits. Sweet, dimpled navel. Faster now, he paddled, thrusting, thrusting, thrusting. He was so close he could touch her. She shrieked. He realized she had been paddling too, but away from him, and he woke coughing. It was hot and his throat was dry. He'd forgotten to switch on the air conditioner. Sweating, he untied his robe at the waist and thought about how the day felt long and tedious and how the plain room smelled like last night's sex. He got up and went to the mirror . . .

Remember, Cleveland, you're the Miracle Baby. The miracle baby boy. You don't remember every detail and how could you? At eighteen weeks, you were born. You weighed less than a can of beans. You were a fighter then, but you didn't know it. No one expected you to live. You had tubes in every orifice and mucus and blood too. You didn't have a chance, and then you did. You weren't a Preemie, you were a Miracle. You are a miracle. You're a survivor. A fighter. You can't lose. Remember . . .

There weren't many fans in the Patong Stadium when he arrived at seven o'clock; the youth fights drew only a few locals. Cleveland had at least an hour until the amateur fights, and then another couple of hours until the money fights. He was always scheduled for ten, but it was usually more like eleven or eleven-thirty when he entered the ring, and by then the stadium was full.

He ordered the same pre-fight meal as usual: Pad Thai, two spring rolls, and roasted chicken. He ate in the back of the stadium, by the entrance to the locker rooms. He liked that back area of the stadium. Black and white photographs of fighters and the crowd and the scenes of a fight night lined the wall. Maybe that was his real wish: to be seen in a black and white still shot. Everyone wants to be seen and remembered like that.

The night he'd asked Anong out on a second date, it was past midnight and he met her outside Suzy Wong's off Bangla road where she'd just finished dancing. Bangla road was neon and excitement and yelling and stumbling and slurring and touching and, since their first date, he had made it a point to meet her at the end of her shift.

Why you come here, to me, every night? she said.

I want to make sure you get to your ride safely, with all of these crazies out here.

She looked around her and paused, then looked at Cleveland and said, *You know what you want?*

They walked together hand-in-hand. Anong was short, much shorter and smaller than Cleveland, but he had difficulty keeping up with her pace. He wanted to ask her if she knew what *she* wanted, but he said, *I just want to take you out for dinner.*

Yes-yes, dinner okay, but I know the man.

Anong's smile was warming and honest and pleading, too. How could she do all of that with just her lips, Cleveland wondered? She had shy, lean eyes. She had a birthmark the shape of a tiny head of broccoli on the inside of her right elbow. He figured she was in her early twenties, and did that mean she was too young to fall for him? Why couldn't the now thirty-something Miracle Baby find love in a young Thai girl? Anything was possible. Men, with varying intentions, hovered over her, Cleveland knew. He felt beads of sweat on his chest and back wetting his shirt even though the heat wasn't stifling that night. *I'd like to see you again.*

You break law? she said.

No.

What you run from then?

Not running, just sort of starting over.

It doesn't start over.

What doesn't?

Nothing.

Cleveland didn't understand what she meant, but understood the resolution in her response. They were cutting through back streets and alleyways.

Your family, she said. *They know you here? For start over.*

America's a little different.

I know. I know the American man, he different. She stopped walking. They were at a street corner and a man in a taxi was waiting for her. *I go now.*

I can see you again?

For you, okay. Dinner okay. You know my price-la, yeah? For the night?

He nodded yes. Her price was 1,000 baht for two hours; 3,000 baht for the night. That was easy for the Miracle Baby.

Why I like you, Anong said to Cleveland on their third date when they watched an Adam Sandler blockbuster flick at the Jungceylon mall cinema, *is because you honest. I see you can't lie. Most foreign man they lie. You never lie me.*

She was direct and simple. Life should be simple. He simply told her after the movie that he wanted to be with her and only her. She said, *okay-la, just don't be jealous me. If you jealous too much, you can't love.*

After finishing his meal, Cleveland wandered through the stadium. He watched the women sparring and shadow-boxing and preparing for their fights. The crowd began to stream in, and then he saw Anong enter with a line of other Thai women, all clad in hot pink bikini tops and loosely flowing sarong dresses wrapped at the waist. His body reeled. The women were escorted to the second level seating. A bell sounded and the first two women fighters took their positions in the ring. Cleveland continued ambling around the stadium floor, casually alternating his attention to the ring and then toward Anong.

The music began: the *sarama*, the traditional Muay Thai music. Men's hands patted and slapped hand drums and tickled the bamboo hand-made flutes and strummed some wild version of a guitar. The women bowed and offered thanks and praise to the gods. It looked more like a dance or a yoga routine. All controlled, there was kneeling and bowing and lunging.

"Oh-ya-yo," a voice behind Cleveland said. "You win tonight?"

He turned. It was Cecilia The Ladyboy, whom Cleveland had known since he began competing in the money fights some three years ago. The son of a famous and aging Thai senator, Cecilia had studied in America, spoke like an American, and had lots of money. He was a regular at the Patong Stadium and a degenerate gambler. A he-she, a transsexual. Make-up and eyeliner thick and moist like silt, C-cup breasts, high heels, deep voice, and a penis taped somewhere against his groin.

"Yeah," Cleveland said, "I'll win."

"You should have another name. Tiger or Lion."

"Por Pramuk is good."

"Baby, he's no match for you."

Cleveland nodded and then Cecilia leaned into him.

"You can do much better than that," Cecilia said, nodding toward the second level where Anong sat.

There had been many girls since Cleveland had been in Asia. He had paid for some of them, but none, he was convinced, was like Anong. Sure, she was beautiful and sexy, but there were a million girls like that, especially in Thailand. He paid for Anong. She grabbed his balls, but yanked his heart. Cleveland felt alive. Finally, obsessed with something other than himself, the Miracle Boy. Wasn't that love?

Cleveland wanted to say *fuck off, already, ladyboy*, but the start bell sounded. They turned to the ring to watch. There was commotion and chatter in the stands, fan banter and side-betting. Cleveland looked again at Anong. She offered a soft, distant smile, and then turned to play with her phone. The rest of the girls around her were the same: bored and unamused with the scene, simply waiting for the rest of the night. Inside, Cleveland was a storm.

Cleveland and Cecilia watched the fight until a group of foreign men entered through the lobby. Cleveland didn't know them, but he knew them: Western business-men. They'd probably just come from work, where they'd made some multinational exchange that loaded their pockets. The men were escorted to the second level and found seats next to and around Anong and her group of girls. The men and women shuffled seats. There were handshakes, hugs, kisses, and touches. Cleveland watched

Anong greet and hug each man and then settle with one who looked like all the rest. Swirling storm of envy and bitterness, winds of want and hatred and lust and greed. And rage.

Cleveland paid Anong for her . . . loyalty. Standing there by the ring, watching, he felt every second. Inside the ring, one girl flung the other to the floor and they squirmed until their bodies intertwined and then one recoiled and they stood again and circled each other until one found room to kick or punch or grab. Cecilia growled and snickered at it all, while Cleveland turned into himself.

After the women fought he returned to the locker room. He took a cold shower and washed and dried himself meticulously. He applied lotion and oil and Tiger Balm and Vaseline. He soaked his mouthpiece. He wore his maroon fighting trunks and his red, white, and blue robe. His mitts were tighter than normal and his hands began to feel numb when he didn't move, jab, swing, or bob them.

A Thai man entered and said, "Oh-ya-yo, go-time soon-soon."

At the front entrance of the locker room where Cleveland had eaten earlier, the music still sang in the background. In the stands, he saw that Anong and the girls and the Western businessmen were seated as couples now: interwoven hands, hips, thighs, and sides moving as one, even though they sat in stiff stadium seats. It was all part of the sleaze. Rich Thai business and governmental men invited Western entrepreneurs and corporations to showcase potential imported goods and discuss deals that would make both sides richer. The local hosts would arrange for after-work activities, which in Phuket meant girls and booze and at least one night of the popular boxing. Cleveland didn't see them every night he fought, but he saw them often enough. He imagined their conversations were stale and abrasive. Anong played along. How far would the night go? Cleveland didn't want to think about that. It was just sex. Wasn't it? Only sex? Sex, sex, sex. She was a ring girl. She was a model. A dancer. Anything she was paid to be. A girlfriend? A wife? She sat next to one of the men. Her right leg straddled his left. If Cleveland looked real close, he could see her crotch slightly open through the sarong. It was night and everything was open. He felt sick, so he bounce-stepped and shuffled his feet as if to warm up. He swung his arms back and forth and punched his face with each hand until he felt nothing except the tightness of his mitts.

A crowd had gathered and continued to stream in. Cleveland noticed a few of the men where Anong sat, pointing to him. *Who's that?* Cleveland imagined them saying. *Oh, that's Oh-ya-yo. He foreigner who fight good-good,* a girl would respond. He was a spectacle to them all, and then he was in the ring.

The musicians played and the crowd cheered and yelled, but he couldn't hear them. Sound waved through his mind like it was a placid, calm lake. Time slowed, space widened: he imagined the Western man in some stale hotel room mounting Anong like a beast and the other girls are there too, and Cecilia The Ladyboy, all watching and the Miracle Baby breaks down the door, throws the man against the wall, and stomps on his crotch and head until Anong, sweet Anong, tells him no more and rushes to his arms.

Por Pramuk was in front of him. Cleveland moved, circling him, waiting, watching until the time was just right. The Tiger Balm he lathered on his face numbed his nose and lips and stung his nostrils. He could see the sweat on Por Pramuk's brow and watched him spit and then grind his teeth on his mouthpiece. Cleveland breathed and drew deeper into himself. I am, he thought, a ravage . . . a ravaging ring rebel . . .

Por Pramuk struck Cleveland first—it was a shin-kick—and the crowd cooed. Ants, Cleveland thought, and he didn't care if they cooed, cried, or called out. They'd all drown. All of them, Cleveland thought, except for Anong. Por Pramuk jabbed a punch at Cleveland's torso, but Cleveland blocked Por Pramuk's fist, leaned in quick and fast, threw his right elbow to Por Pramuk's chin and then wailed a left jab to his temple. *Oh-ya-yo* . . .

By the end of round one, Cleveland was straddling Por Pramuk and drilling his mitts into the man's skull. For Cleveland, it felt syrupy. The bell had already rung. The musicians stopped playing. The crowd yelled in horror. The referees pried Cleveland off Por Pramuk and called the fight. Por Pramuk lay, bloodied and still, in the middle of the ring. It'd happened so fast. Cleveland looked to the crowd and saw Cecilia The Ladyboy's makeup sliding off her sweating face. The stadium smelled like metallic blood and rancid cooking oil and spilled Chang beer. He looked to the second level seats, but didn't see Anong. He was grabbed and handled. He felt swollen and heavy. It was a deep, oceanic sensation, like he was being dragged. He let go. There was rabid yelling. Shoving. Shouting. Pointing hands. *You! You! You!* Afflicted and soured. He watched. *You! You! You!* No longer *Oh-ya-yo!* He didn't understand how, but the referees helped him move through the mob to the back of the stadium and into the locker room. "Stay-stay here, yes," one of them said. It wasn't a question. The referee slammed the door shut.

Cleveland scanned the room. His gym bag was in the corner and the white walls began to shrink. Lockers rusty red. The room smelled of damp towels and rubbing alcohol. He heard frantic voices on the other side of the door in the hallway. Fast-talking Thai voices trying to push in. There was a knock.

"Oh-ya-yo," a voice said, and then Anong entered,

unrelenting, a gust of potency and might. "You-you," she said, "you, murderer." She slammed the door shut again.

"Why are you here, with those men?" Cleveland said. He felt the sweaty hair follicles on his torso and around his navel and genitals burning, burning, burning.

"No. You no talk now. You murderer now. You must go."

"Murderer?"

"Por Pramuk. You hit him too much-much in the face. He die."

"He can't be dead." He tore the tape that held his boxing mitts and used his mouth to pull off each glove. He felt Anong's stare settling on him. "It was just a fight."

"You just like other foreigner man. I know. I see now."

"What—"

"I see now."

"No, I'm not."

"Yes-yes. You too strong. You push too hard. You not even care. That worst part. You no love me. Life. Nothing."

"Anong, I didn't mean to hurt him." Slowly Cleveland recounted the fight . . . maybe it was true. Could he have killed a man?

"Now, you lie me. I see you look me upstairs."

"Yeah, I saw you with *that* man."

"I tell you don't jealous me. You can't love when you jealous too much."

"I'm not jealous."

"Now you lie me again."

"You know what's in my bag? I have a ring for you. For you to marry me. You see, I'm not like the others."

"Marry? You think I marry you now? You lie me twice and you kill Por Pramuk. He family outside waiting you and you think about marry me. You jealous too much."

Distance settled between them in the shrinking room. He undressed. She watched him, arms crossed and stern. He covered himself with a towel and the robe he'd brought from the hotel.

"Nothing, see?" she said.

"Nothing what?"

"Nothing can start over. I tell you."

The door was kicked open then. Cleveland saw four Thai men, each carrying something that could whip or beat or strike. The men pushed Anong to the side.

"Hey," Cleveland said. He thought to stand to strike, but he was struck first in the jaw by one of the men, who threw a beer bottle at him. His mind floated then, like he was drunk. It was another type of numbness. He let go.

The men grabbed and punched Cleveland. He fell. One of the men poured a liquid on Cleveland's face, maybe turpentine or some sort of vanish solution, that slid down his throat and he gagged. Three men kicked his sides. Another held him down harder and meaner like Cleveland was a wild hog. The man yelled, "Oh-ya-yo, I kill you now," and then he dug his knuckles into Cleveland's sternum.

Cleveland felt like the man was trying to rip his heart out. He squirmed enough that he loosened himself from the man's hold, and turning on his side then, with breath heaving and reeking of turpentine, he saw the loose, silky sarong that draped Anong's lower half and wondered if she would leave him now. Let it all go. For good. Wet leather whipped him in the kidney, and he rolled on his back to shield that pain. It was almost done, he thought, and then a woman jumped atop his body. She was bony, not plump. Frail almost. He watched her squeeze his neck. The color of her skin was darker than Anong's, which was like a milky latte. Adorned by gold on her fingers and wrists, the woman was not a killer, Cleveland thought. She must be an angry wife and mother, a sister even.

It stopped as it had started. Another fast-speaking Thai voice emerged through the door, a man's voice, and said something and then the room sighed and breathed again. Cleveland heard the thud of the men's weapons dropping to the floor. The woman tiptoed around Cleveland as if it hadn't happened. He watched feet leave the room.

"What," Cleveland said. "What is it?" It was silent then. "Is he dead," he said, "Oh, God . . . Is he really dead?"

He didn't hear Anong approach, but he saw her above him; he felt like she floated there.

"It miracle he not dead," she said. "You lucky."

He exhaled. "See, I told you." He wanted to reach for her, but didn't. He couldn't. "Everything's fine. Let's go get your money. Just help me to an ATM. We can sleep in and go tomorrow—"

"No, no." She waved her finger at him. "Nothing same now. Your money is no good. You no good. I know man like you, I tell you. I only there with the men to helping Kanda. I wasn't going to have naughty with them. I liked you, but . . . " She walked away from him.

"Wait, where are you going?"

She retrieved his gym bag and sat it by his side. "You take your ring and leave now. Okay-la?" She lowered her face to his and kissed him, this time on the forehead, as if it was a final, last action. A final goodbye, perhaps. Cleveland wasn't sure about anything. Maybe he never had been. She closed the door shut and left the stadium.

Cleveland took his time getting up. He hobbled and stumbled. There was an eerie silence that was still and staged, as if someone were taking his picture. He ran the shower, but could hardly stand still under the frigid water. He put on swim trunks and a white tank top. He laced and tied his running shoes. It was well past midnight. Leaving the gym bag with the ring there in the tiny-laced sack, he walked out of the locker room and passed the boxing ring and exited through the lobby and out of the Patong stadium. He continued walking with the same steady pace through the parking lot and headed west, toward Bangla road. He didn't stop. Through the side streets he marched like he knew where he was. He followed his senses: *satays* flaming on the makeshift street grills, vendors squeezing colorful tropical fruits until they were suffocated rinds and peels, passing tuk-tuks thumping and bouncing bass and blasting hip-hop music from speakers the drivers could hardly afford.

When he finally reached Bangla road, the neon lights reminded him of cotton candy. Bangla road was alive and bare and gyrating and wiggling. He stopped at one of the long, open-air main street bars with the high ceilings, stripper poles on every table, and strippers pranced on every surface, sometimes hugging, kissing each other. Men groveled and begged for the women like they were starving. All the flesh didn't faze Cleveland. Music pounding so hard. He sat at a bar and ordered *sang som*.

"You funny man," the waitress said.

"Yes," Cleveland said. "Very funny."

"What happen you? You fight?"

"I got beat up."

"Oh," she said, and poured him another whiskey. "This one free. You okay?"

"I deserved it."

To his right, five or six barstools down, a dancer—likely on her break, Cleveland thought—ate fried grasshoppers from a small, plastic baggy. He motioned for her, and she came immediately.

"Yes?" she said.

"Can I have one?"

She looked back toward her seat at the bar. "You want grasshopper?"

"Yes," Cleveland said. "I want grasshopper."

"Oh, yes-yes," she said and smiled. She retrieved the bag and stood even closer to Cleveland, pushing her crotch to his side.

"You want this?"

Cleveland nodded yes.

She took one grasshopper and sucked on it so half of it protruded from her mouth.

"I can take it?" Cleveland said.

She nodded yes and moved her face toward his.

Their lips touched, hers wetter than his, and Cleveland steadied himself there, sucking either the head or the abdomen of the insect, he wasn't sure which. She let go first, and while still chewing her half of the bug, she kissed Cleveland again on his lips.

"You can have everything you want," she said.

"I can have those," he said, gesturing toward the bag.

"Yes. Okay-la, no problem. You take me too?"

He thought about Anong. "No, doll," he said. He'd never said *doll* in that way before. "Not tonight."

He stood. Sweat beads cooled his skin. The *sang som* diluted the turpentine that still lingered in his throat. He realized he had no money on him, so he promised the waitress he'd return the next day to pay for the whiskey.

"Okay," she said. "No problem. You go rest-rest, yes?"

He thanked the dancer, the one he called doll, for sharing her grasshoppers. She tried to reach for him, but he retreated.

"Oh," she said. "What problem? You no want me? Let's make naughty funny-funny."

"I'm already too funny." He smiled at her. She looks like Anong, he thought. Maybe she was Anong. "Next time," he said, reaching out to touch her glimmering skin. Then he turned and walked to the middle of Bangla road with the plastic baggy of fried grasshoppers in his hand.

The rest of that night he ran through the streets and side streets and along the beach pathways and back alleyways of Phuket. He stopped and walked when he needed. He sat too, when his body ached. The beach breeze of the night air felt good. That's what he loved most about Thailand: the breeze in the nighttime. It reminded him that a new day was near. He came to the end of one street and looked out at the sea before him. Far out, high-beamed lights stretched across the horizon. He walked to the beach and collapsed on the cool sand. He looked again out to the lights. They were the safety and night lights of tankers and rigs that drilled the bottom of the sea floor to suck out black oil. Am I the rig or the oil, Cleveland thought. He wasn't sure he cared, really, or if it mattered. Either way, it was a miracle, wasn't it, how he always survived? You can't lose. Remember, he thought.

He surrendered like that until daybreak, when the morning sky looked like God had vomited all of the most vibrant colors in the world right there for him, and then he swam in the tepid ocean water that felt like velvet on his flesh and the smell of the water reminded him of pickle juice.

"W.W.K.D."

I met Khoudia in my sophomore year, just after Mom died. She was a new student who arrived sometime in January. She was one of only a handful of African students at our international school in Beijing and the only one in Yu *laoshi*'s Advanced Chinese class.

It was a Monday in February when I returned to school. Outside, the sky was thick gray and you could taste the soggy, metallic air, typical during those long Beijing winters. I had on one of mom's wool cardigans, like I always wore then. Yu *laoshi* told me to sit next to Khoudia. She told me I needed to get to know her and welcome her to our school. At first, I thought it was some kind of charity case gesture that teachers tended to ask of their best students. Back then I was always called on to do those types of tasks. I smiled at Yu *laoshi* with approval and said *hao de*.

Khoudia was skinny, but her shoulders were muscular like a boy's. Her neck was long and defined, like it was protecting whatever she was about to say until she said it. When I sat next to her, she smiled and said "hi" with a sailing giddiness in her voice. Her black eyes shone. This wasn't the first time I'd sat next to or even befriended a black student, but this was the first time I had met someone like Khoudia.

"Khoudia," Yu *laoshi* said.

Khoudia sighed, looked at Yu *laoshi*, and said, "That's not my name," in perfect, fluid Chinese.

All the air in the class was gone then. No one spoke to Yu *laoshi* like that.

"*Ni shuo shenme*," Yu *laoshi* said, *what did you say.*

Khoudia sat a little straighter and her elbow accidentally nudged mine. I looked to see if some of her had rubbed off on me.

"My name," Khoudia said. "It's not *Ku-dya*. The K-h is silent. It's *Who-dya*."

There were a few sniggers and sneers, but then Yu *laoshi* frowned and the room went silent again. Yu *laoshi* was always strict, stern, and precise, the type of teacher every student feared.

She cleared her throat and said, "Khoudia," this time pronouncing it as Khoudia requested, "*Gen wo chu lai.*"

Khoudia took her time gazing left and then right, staring us all down, like she was officially introducing herself: *I'm Khoudia and don't get it twisted.* She stood. "Sure," she said, but in English. Yu *laoshi* never permitted her students to speak in English. I could feel her heels stab the floor as she followed Khoudia outside the classroom into the hallway.

At least *Who-dya* isn't boring, I thought. She was something real.

They weren't gone long and when they returned it felt like I was in the middle of something churning. Yu *laoshi* gave us more homework than I'd ever had. I didn't care though, I always got A's.

So did Khoudia. We only had Chinese class and homeroom together, but I saw the red A's scribbled on her papers when Yu *laoshi* returned them, and Chinese was by far the hardest class in tenth grade. I was never nearly as engaged in my other classes just because I didn't have to be, but I still got A's.

Take English, for example. Mr. Loynes tried to be funny which usually just came out corny. At the end of class, he always said, "I hope the rest of your day is as awesome as I am." He was one of those teachers who turned the other cheek when students were a little late to class or late turning in assignments, as long as you had a reason. Mr. Loynes was our homeroom teacher too.

One morning in early March, I was the first to arrive to homeroom. It was before eight and barely light outside. The heavy smog was smothering the sun, suffocating the sky.

"Looks gruesome out, huh, Joanne," Mr. Loynes said

when he entered.

My head was down, but I wasn't sleeping. I had wrapped the black scarf Mom gave me, the one frayed at each end, tight around my neck. I was staring into space. No stars, no moons. Just darkness, but I could breathe.

"You all right today?" Mr. Loynes said.

I sat up kind of hurried. "Yeah, just tired."

"Tired? Come on." His voice sounded like a revving engine. "The day's just getting started. No time for tired."

I played with my iPhone. I wasn't into Angry Bird or Clumsy Ninja, so I googled "Khoudia meaning."

"A lot of homework last night?" Mr. Loynes said, full of coffee and perk.

I nodded. There was nothing convincing I could find out about Khoudia's name. Just before I set my phone down, I looked at the screen background picture of Mom, the one I took from the funeral. Had I ever really known her?

Mr. Loynes pulled out a chair and sat in front of me then. I could feel his tone changing and knew what was coming. "You know," he said, "my step-mom died of breast cancer when I was about your age."

I gave him nothing.

He tried to find my eyes. "It was really tough to watch my dad go through all that."

I coiled strands of my hair that fell by my cheekbone—it was a habit I had—and looked at the framed picture on his desk. To his right, a man, lanky and blond, like Mr.

Loynes, probably his brother, and to his left, a freckle-faced white woman. They were in a jungle somewhere, maybe Indonesia, maybe Thailand, an orangutan in the background.

"You know, if you ever need to talk," he said, letting each word linger in the empty classroom, "or anything, I want you to know, I'm here for you."

I didn't say anything. The other students started arriving then.

Back when we lived in San Francisco, Mom and Dad both traveled all the time for work. He was a mechanical engineer for Audi. Mom was a corporate lawyer. Then Dad got the big raise he'd been waiting for and the relocation assignment to Beijing. I was ten.

"It's just for a few years," he said.

The way he said that made me think he and Mom had known about this move for a long time.

I said I didn't want to leave. I liked my school, my friends.

"*Tian Tian*," Mom said, she liked to call me that, "it will be good for you. We'll have opportunities there you can't possibly have here. Plus, you need to improve your Chinese."

When we moved to Beijing, we visited Grandma and Grandpa in Taiwan every chance we got. Dad traveled so much it seemed like I only saw him when we had a holiday, and there we were again in Taipei, at Grandma's house sipping oolong tea and eating mooncake.

After a few years, Mom got bored. She had joined the PTA at school, but she wanted something more, I know now. She was too smart for the PTA. Back in San Francisco, she had been really successful. Later, I even found out, she was offered partnership at her firm, but didn't take it so Dad could take his promotion. One night at dinner she started talking about a professorship opening at NTU in Taipei and then she said, "I want to go back to work."

Dad hardly flinched. He dug his chopsticks in a plate of chow mein.

"I can teach a few classes during the week," Mom said, "and fly back on the weekends."

Just like before, I knew the decision had already been made.

I was in eighth grade then and had long been earning the highest marks in my class.

"*Tian Tian*," Mom said, "what do you think?"

What did I think? I was thirteen. I could tell Mom wanted this—maybe more than me—and I wasn't going to disappoint her. "It's fine," I said, but really, I just wanted Mom.

I should have seen the signs. Her visits back to Beijing were less and less frequent. She may have started out teaching law, but then the cancer took over and she was at the hospital, becoming paler and skinnier and losing handfuls of her long dark hair that was just like mine. I didn't know.

Khoudia was Muslim. She brought it up in Yu *laoshi's* class during our unit study on World Religions. It was April and Beijing was beginning to warm. Khoudia talked about the upcoming Tabaski holiday that celebrated Abraham's willingness to sacrifice his son Ishmael for God.

This boy Billy Chen, who thought he knew everything, interrupted Khoudia and asked if there were Islamist terrorists in Senegal like in the rest of the world. There were some *oohs* and *aahs*, but Yu *laoshi* let it slide.

Khoudia sucked her teeth. "No," she said and went on to explain how Senegal was a country of mostly Muslims but the president was Christian, and how Muslims and Christians married each other and celebrated each other's holidays as if they were one. She said her people were African before they were religious. "One day," Khoudia said, "I'll be the president of Senegal."

The class laughed, but I never thought otherwise.

Later that day we had a school-wide assembly to discuss the upcoming Week Without Walls trips. Khoudia and I sat next to each other.

"I hate that boy Billy," she said.

I looked at her.

"You, too?"

"Yeah," I said, "he is a—"

"Cunt," Khoudia said. I had never heard anyone actually say that word in public. Not *that* word. Khoudia continued: "And a dick. Billy Chen is a cunt-dick."

It was absurd and dirty and true. I laughed and then Khoudia laughed, and then the principal asked everyone to stop talking, but Khoudia and I were still laughing. She grabbed my arm. It felt good.

Later, after we'd stopped laughing and the principal was still yapping about how *amazing* these trips were going to be, Khoudia said, "Have you ever eaten lamb?"

"Lamb?"

"You want to come over this weekend for Tabaski? It'll be fun. Come on."

I hadn't laughed like that in a long time. "Sure."

"Great," Khoudia said, "it'll be *amazing*."

Khoudia's father was a diplomat so they lived inside the 3rd Ring road, where most of the embassies were located. She wore a long, lavender-colored dress that hugged her skinny frame. It was embroidered with magnificent golden patterns stitched on the sleeves and along the tail of the dress, which dangled to the ground. She moved so freely and effortlessly. I felt underdressed in my yellow spring dress. The day was crisp and sunny. Khoudia's father's smile fell into his face and the whites of his eyes were sharp and hypnotizing. "Joanne," he said, "please, our home is your home. Welcome." I understood Khoudia better then.

She took my hand and led me through the house that eventually emptied into a beautiful courtyard. Tall and sprawling plants and shrubs hugged the path and spilled over the top of the property's walls. Men and women and children, all dressed as magnificently as Khoudia, talked and laughed and swayed about the yard. I didn't know that many Africans even lived in Beijing.

A few men with dreadlocks banged on drums that hung at their waists. Another man sat huddled over a hand-carved xylophone and another strummed what looked like a guitar. Khoudia pulled me to dance. Everyone danced. I heard voices that were not Chinese or English, words that made sounds that floated and soared and leapt, that were of another world where I imagined people had wings like butterflies and the sky was always turquoise and warm.

We sat in a circle, joined by a few older women, on a large tapestry. Some minutes later a silver platter, covered with yellow rice, chunks of lamb meat, steamed carrots, and bell peppers, was lowered before us. Along the edges, grilled lamb chops and French bread.

I waited for a prayer, but one of the women pulled rice from the platter with her hand and began eating and then we all followed. Rice smeared my hands and dress. The meat was tender and tasted like it had been marinated in vinegar. I listened to Khoudia and the women talk in their language. There was nothing I could contribute, but I wished I could give them something. "Khoudia," I finally said. "Which one is your mom?"

Khoudia looked around the circle and then at me. She took another lump of rice and lamb meat, rolled it in her hand, and before she put it in her mouth she said, "*Sama yaay* died a long time ago."

My heart sank a little then.

There was more celebration after dinner. More music and dancing. The moon lit the night sky, and we stayed there on the lawn until there were only a few of us remaining.

That night, lying in one of the twin beds in Khoudia's room, I dreamed about San Francisco—the same dream I always have. We're on our street in our neighborhood, and it's the moment when I realize I can ride a bicycle all by myself. I always wake at the same time, too. It's right when Dad gives me one last shove and my handlebars are wobbling down the street. Dad's yelling *Jia You!* and I hear Mom say, "Strong and steady, *Tian Tian*, stay strong and steady." I'm on my own riding away and I wake up just before I fall.

"Whose is this?" Khoudia said.

It was a few weeks after Tabaski and a school gym bag was on her desk that wasn't hers. This wasn't unusual. Theft at our affluent school was virtually unheard of, so stuff was left everywhere. I was reading *The Wind-Up Bird Chronicle,* waiting for everyone else to arrive. I shrugged.

"Not sure," I said and kept reading. I was at the part where Toru is in Tokyo sitting outside a donut shop, watching passersby.

Khoudia played with the tags at the top of the bag. "Oh," she said.

I looked at her then.

"It's Billy Chen's gym bag." Khoudia's long fingers played with the zipper. "Let's see how we can terrorize him."

"LOL," I said.

She rummaged through and said, "Eww, look." She shoved her body and the bag toward me.

It was just typical stinky, sweaty high school boy gym bag stuff. Sneakers, shorts, wrist band, socks, but it was Billy Chen's, so it smelled like cunt-dick. "Gross," I said.

"Well, well," Khoudia said, "what do we have here?" She took a pencil, reached in the bag, and lifted out a bundle of royal blue rubber W.W.J.D. bracelets. Everyone had one of those bracelets back then.

Khoudia smirked. "Aha! Even more proof he's a fraud."

I knew what Khoudia meant. Billy Chen was really a jerk and so he couldn't be a Christian like his bracelet claimed. Mr. Loynes wanted me to know I could talk to him, but I could tell he said that to make himself feel better. Yu *laoshi* was strict and stern, sure, but let's face it, she was just a teacher who gave out a lot of homework. Dad was a successful engineer, but he didn't know how to talk to me. Mom called me her sweet, her *Tian Tian*, and said she loved me, but I didn't believe that either. Everything then felt like a fraud except for Khoudia.

She went into her backpack and pulled out a black Sharpie. "He needs an intervention."

I nodded.

Khoudia wrote over the "J" with a "K."

"What Would Khoudia Do?" I said.

"Damn straight."

Mr. Loynes entered the room then. Khoudia dropped the bracelet in the bag and zipped it closed.

"Aoooooooooo," Mr. Loynes howled. "Two days, ladies! Two days!"

Khoudia rolled her eyes one way, and I rolled mine the other.

"A A Aooooooooooo," he said again. "Are you ready for the wild, Khoudia? The great outdoors, Joanne?"

Khoudia shot him a look.

"Either way," Mr. Loynes said, "the wild is ready for you." He started to stand in a tree pose then.

"Mr. Loynes," Khoudia said, "I think we should be able to take our cellphones at least because—"

"Nope. No cellphone, no laptop. The only thing electronic with us on the trail will be a battery-operated GPS that you will have to read to make sure we're going the right way. Can't get lost in the wild, Khoudia. Otherwise, you know what'll happen. Aaaaaooooooooooo."

"What if it rains?" Khoudia said.

"Rain! We would only be so lucky!"

The rest of the class trickled in then. Mr. Loynes projected maps and pictures of our destination. Some wilderness organization our school hired came in and showed us how to track and follow GPS coordinates, how to put up a tent, how to cook on a camp stove. They handed out pens and leather-bound journals with thick paper.

"We want you to take full advantage out there," the camp director said. "Immerse yourself in the wilderness. You'll be challenged, but you'll be better for it."

He went on and on about what we had to pack, what we could and couldn't eat, every what if scenario he could think of. Khoudia slipped me a note: *This is so lame.* I drew a mountain with a line of stick figures leaping off the ledge. One of the figures yelled *Yep!* in a speech balloon.

The program director continued. He was shorter than Mr. Loynes and every piece of clothing he wore had some sort of nifty zipper. "We're going out there with a 'Leave No Trace' mentality." From his big backpacker's bag, he took out a hand-held shovel, a roll of toilet paper, and a bundle of plastic baggies. "We can't leave any trace of our being out there in the wilderness. And I mean nothing."

The class looked around at each other.

Khoudia looked at me. "What?"

I shrugged.

"If you go number two," he finally said, "it's coming back with you." He held up the shovel and toilet paper like it was all some type of religious ceremony. It was chaos in the classroom then.

"Excuse me," Khoudia said. "No way I'm picking up my poop and carrying it around for a week."

"All in the experience, Khoudia," Mr. Loynes said. "All in the experience. Aaaaaoooooooooo!"

We left early from school on a Saturday morning. An hour out of Beijing, the highway was lined with smokestacks spewing out exhaust from factories. Khoudia, who was sitting next to me, fell asleep. What Mom said in my dream kept coming back to me: *Stay strong and steady*. I was always strong and steady, just like her. The thing is, I never knew Mom was sick, so how could her death feel real. She didn't want me there by her side cheering her on to stay strong and steady despite it all. She didn't want me to see her sick, and I understood that, but I never got to say goodbye. That's what hurt the worst: so many things left unsaid. I looked around the bus. Everyone was sleeping. I tried to finish reading my book, but finally dozed off too.

It was a three-hour drive just to reach a tiny village that was our starting point. There were twelve of us, plus Mr. Loynes and the camp program director, who told us to call him Mr. Chris. We only spotted a few elders, who either stared at us like we were Martians or smiled at us with crooked or missing teeth and sun-worn faces. After we passed through the village, the path tightened and ascended. We walked steadily at first: Mr. Chris at the front, Mr. Loynes at the back. We walked single-file, pushing branches and thorns out of the way, our breathing as burdensome as our backpacks. We nursed on water from our CamelBak hydration packs. We stopped every fifteen or twenty minutes, and then, as the trek steepened, we walked more slowly up the stubborn mountainside.

After a while, Khoudia said, "Okay, that's it. I can't go anymore." We must have hiked two or three hours. She plopped down on the path, leaning her backpack against a tree root. The terrain had become more rocky and less dusty, the trees more rooty, angular, and piney.

We all followed Khoudia. We were tired teenagers, thinking about our iPhones and KFC. Mr. Chris came back down the path and Mr. Loynes caught up from the end of the line.

"Good job, gang," Mr. Loynes said. He still stood, tall and lanky, only sweating a little. "I think we're making good time."

Mr. Chris wasn't as optimistic. "We're going to want to push forward. Get to the top before it gets dark."

"The top?" Khoudia said. "The top of what? Doesn't look like there's a top."

"It's beautiful up there," Mr. Chris said. "Just you wait

and see."

"Um, spoiler alert! I've already seen it. Mr. Loynes showed us pictures last week, remember?"

We were all too tired to react.

"Let's remember the three R's," Mr. Chris said. He looked at us with his stupid enthusiasm.

"Jesus," Khoudia said under her breath. "Can I just have a cracker or something?"

"Re-energize, Re-hydrate, Re-immerse," he said. His voice heightened. He had the face of somebody selling something used.

I looked down at my dusky boots and thought about Toru Okada being stuck there in his well, trying to figure out everything.

The top was worth it. There were waves of thick grass and springing wildflowers and trees tall and wide enough to climb and hide in. We were on a plateau and finally could stop hiking for the day.

"Okay everyone," Mr. Chris said. We were huddled in a circle, our backpacks thrown on the ground. "Take a few minutes to let this all soak in. Look around you. The trees. The green. The blue sky you can reach out and touch. The cliffs there. Look! They're sprouting above the clouds, like they're daring whatever greater Higher Being you believe in."

We all looked around. Mr. Loynes didn't say anything

silly then although I think we were all expecting it. There was a whispering breeze, and I tried to remember Mom's voice.

"Go, explore," Mr. Chris said. "Be one in—" and then he waited and looked at us, like he wanted us to fill in the blank. " . . . The wilderness. Be one with the wilderness. With the world. Ten minutes. Go!"

Khoudia took my hand and we walked to the side of the plateau where the sun was setting. The sky was a collage of orange and magenta and blue. I followed Khoudia along the ridge and then we found a rock along a shallow path big enough for both of us. We sat and she immediately took out two candy bars.

"Snickers?" I said. "Where'd you get—"

"I'm not eating dried fruit and granola bars every day. I got a whole bag of them. Twix bars too." Her giggling rushed over the plateau's edge.

She ravaged the wrapper, broke the bar in half, and gave me one. I didn't hesitate to lick the oozing, melted caramel. I looked at Khoudia and then peered over the edge from where we sat on the rock. I couldn't see through the thick, misty clouds. We were above everything.

"I was too late to see my mom," I said.

We didn't have much time, I knew.

"Say what?" Khoudia said.

"My mom." I took a bite then. "When I found out she was sick—really sick—my dad and I went to the airport to board a plane to Taipei. By that time, she was staying at my grandma and grandpa's house."

Khoudia didn't say anything.

"Grandpa met us at the airport. Mom died while we were flying over the Taiwan Strait, while I was watching *The Girl with the Dragon Tattoo* dubbed over in Chinese." I tried to cry to prove to the mountains I loved Mom, but I was dry.

"Oh," Khoudia said. She had one more bite of Snickers in her hand. I knew she wanted to eat it, but she waited. The breeze got heavier. "I'm sorry," she said.

I just kept looking out into the sea of mist, imagining it would feel like a soft blanket.

"My mom," Khoudia said. She waited for me to look at her. "She—"

We heard a whistle then in the distance. "Return to the circle," Mr. Chris was yelling out to everyone. "We have to set camp and get the fire going before it gets dark. Come back everyone!"

"Your mom what?" I said to Khoudia.

She popped the last of the Snickers in her mouth. "She died after she had me. Hospitals in Senegal are a nightmare."

"Oh," I said, "I just thought—I didn't—"

"It's all right," Khoudia said. "Like I said, it was a long, long time ago."

I wondered how Khoudia cried, what her tears looked

like.

"What was your mom like?" Khoudia said.

"What do you mean?"

"Your mom. Tell me about her—"

Mr. Chris was blowing the whistle again and yelling.

I could feel Khoudia looking at me. I could only come up with: "I guess she looks like me."

"You mean you look like her. I look like *sama yaay* too. That's the thing about moms: they follow us wherever we go, no matter what."

I hoped Khoudia was right. We got up from the rock then and joined the others.

The next few days were much the same: early wake-up call, take down the tent, breakfast, hike until lunch, eat tortillas smeared with peanut butter and a can of tuna fish, journal about how much we loved nature and all that crap Mr. Chris was selling, hike again after lunch up and down all through the Chinese wilderness, set up camp, cook and eat dinner, sleep.

On the morning of the last day, Mr. Chris got all sappy. We were huddled in a circle, like we'd been doing every time he had something to say to the group. "Today is it," he said. "You'll return to your laptop and I-gadgets and face the real world again."

"Not the real world!" Mr. Loynes said. His face was long, his mouth ajar. "Someone will have to teach me how to turn on my Macbook, check my email. Oh, the horror!"

"We're not done yet, Mr. Loynes," Mr. Chris said, commanding our attention again. "We have one . . . more . . . challenge."

"Jesus," Khoudia said, again under her breath. "Why is he always so dramatic?"

"You have two hours," Mr. Chris continued, "all by yourself. I like to call it Alone Time."

We looked around at each other, contemplating our first move to escape.

"There's no way to get out of this one and, believe me, students have tried. Now, everyone stand up and turn around with your back to the inside of the circle. Let's go, up and move, everybody."

We all stood and did like he said. Khoudia was to my right.

Mr. Chris continued: "When I say go, you'll walk straight ahead for seven minutes. I'll time you. After seven minutes, I'll blow the whistle and you'll stop, find a place to sit, and just . . . be . . . alone." He was on the outside of the circle now, pacing, making eye contact, like he was a drill sergeant. "When I say go, do not stop walking. I repeat, do not stop walking. It is very foggy this morning. Trust me, you will not see your neighbor and your neighbor will not see you. You'll want to run and find a friend, but I advise you not to do this. Stay with the discomfort. Stay with the wilderness. I'll be circling through the area, making sure you're alone."

Khoudia squeezed my hand twice, like it was code. I squeezed hers three times.

"Ready?" Mr. Chris said, and after a few seconds, he yelled, "Go!"

The walk was just like he said. I could barely see five feet in front of me. The ground was soft. The air was cool and moist. I felt like I had been walking forever, and then I heard the whistle blow in the distance behind me. I looked around at nothing but mist and one lonely tree a few feet from me. I heard nothing but the same forest crackling sounds I'd been hearing the last few days. I walked to the tree and sat at the foot of it, on top of a patch of moss that ran around the base of the trunk. Dampness soaked through my pants, but I didn't care. I leaned my head back against the tree, closed my eyes, and fell asleep.

When I woke I thought for sure it'd been at least two hours. There was a rustling coming in the distance to the left. I heard Khoudia whisper, "Joanne," through the foggy, wet air. "Khoudia?" I said. "Over here." I didn't stand though. I didn't want to. I just wanted to sit with Mom.

"I got to go."

"Where?"

"No. I mean. I have to go! Bad!" Her eyes spelled out each word. "I think I ate too many candy bars."

There was another rustling then.

"Oh, shit," Khoudia said, "That's Mr. Chris," and she dashed through the fog again.

It didn't take long before I fell in and out of sleep again, like my life was all a dream. There was Mom smiling. She told me it was okay. I hugged her and cried. Finally, I cried. When I woke, some of the fog had cleared atop the plateau. I looked at my feet. There was a caterpillar on my boot. It didn't have the faintest idea. I was watching it move so quickly and without inhibitions. I felt a little like God for a minute and then remembered I had to hike downhill later that day. I made a bridge with my finger for the caterpillar and it propelled its way onto the moss.

The whistle blew again in the distance. Alone Time was over for now. When we all returned to camp everyone looked a little squeamish and tired. Mr. Chris and Mr. Loynes had hot chocolate ready for us. I saw Khoudia. She was grinning hard, like she pooped somewhere in the woods where she knew Mr. Chris would step in it someday. I took my cup over to where she stood.

"Well, I don't know about you," she said, "but I'm ready to leave all this wilderness."

"Damn straight," I said.

Sometime, long ago, I was in our back yard, back in San Francisco, with Mom. This was my favorite photo—the one I took a picture of with my iPhone and have since saved on every electronic device I've ever had. It's an old photograph, curved now around its white edges and more grainy than photographs today. Dad was snapping shots of Mom and me. Mom is pushing me in the swing and I can feel the day like it was yesterday. The sun's bright and strong, but not brighter or stronger than her. She looks just like me. I look just like her. She's pushing me on the swing until my tummy burns warm and then Dad says, *Women chi ba,* and Mom makes us peanut butter and jelly sandwiches. She cuts the edges of my bread because I can't stand the texture of the crust and she braids my hair in pigtails while I eat. The grass is green and the air is turquoise and it's warm and the butterflies are singing. *Tian Tian,* Mom says, I love you always. You're my *Tian Tian,* my *baobei,* my *meimei.* I smile and will smile forever at Mom. It was sometime, long long ago.

"BUCKET LIST"

I should go to my *own* bedroom. The shining sun makes me want to tear out my eyeballs, but I don't want to move. Not just yet. I'm pretty sure that's my sequined black minidress with the slits down its back hanging on Amy's closet door but it doesn't matter; all our clothes are all over the place anyway. That's how we've been living lately, me and Amy. We're roommates who happen to have the same name.

I don't understand Amy's body temperature, but whatevs. I'm lying next to her, and she's wrapped herself in her white IKEA duvet like she wants to mummify. It's way too hot for 6:13 in the morning. And anyway, it smells like sweaty pubic hairs and liquor. Have you smelled sweaty pubic hairs before? I should really light a candle or something.

On the floor I see the size-seven red high heels that we can both wear and then there are the white jeans that are too tight for me but look good on Amy. They sit on her hips like they're her hips and doesn't that just make you jealous as fuck? Sometime last night she tossed her panties on the three-legged armchair in the corner. They're sheer granny-panties and read *Lick Me* at the crotch in hot pink. They were a gag gift I gave her on Valentine's along with a pair of cock socks. On the nightstand there are two half-full glasses of Coke Zero and who knows whose is whose? We share it all, me and Amy.

Borgen Kuznetsov left like an hour ago.

What a name. What an idiot. When he woke, he rummaged around our apartment saying, "Where is it, where is it," which sounded like *vair eez eet, vair eez eet,* and then he cursed at us in Russian. What a dumbass. Amy would say the same. She's sort of snoring in her cocoon and it's cute as hell. I told Borgen I didn't have *it,* which isn't true. It was his fault though. He should've never messed with the Attacking Amys of Chaoyang. We're expats living in Beijing.

Last night, Amy and I had dinner and wine with Honey and Jade at Element Fresh, moved on to cocktails at Mosto and then we all got bored and ended up at a table in the back corner at Chocolate. On the stage, this Chinese guy was doing The Robot. Later, some Nigerian guy got on the microphone and called for "all the ladies who got junk in the trunk" to join in a Twerk-a-thon on stage. That didn't last long. After, DJ Knee How blasted hip hop and everyone danced. I'd been ready to go home since

Mosto, but I never know how to tell Amy.

When DJ Knee How came on, the Goon Squad came in. There were, like, ten of them: big, bulky, Incredible Hulk-like man-boys with crew cuts. Muscles are so overrated. These tools wore tight red T-shirts that literally read *Goon Squad* on the front. On the back was their Russian flag: one horizontal red stripe being humped by a blue stripe, being humped by a white stripe.

A flag says a lot about how its people hump.

It wasn't clear what the big deal was about this group of goons, but the gossip Jade overheard was that it was a team of gold medalists from the Track and Field World Championships, which were being held out at the Bird's Nest. It was an Olympic qualifier event. Sure enough, each goon was wearing a gold medal that looked more dull than gold in the strobe light-lit, smoky club.

Amy and I met Borgen by way of force on the dance floor, which was *his* bad. First, he came behind Amy and tried to grind on her. There was nothing subtle about it. Borgen waved his medal in the air and yelled, "*Eey vin eet vor ahsses, eey muhst haav ahsses.*" I'd been dancing *with* Amy, facing her, which meant I got a full frontal of Borgen.

Amy's Chinese-American, but really she's more, like, American-Chinese. She's a little shorter than me. Midnight hair. Firm, slim body. C breasts. She's got a mole on her lip. We've been roommates for almost a year, but started fooling around every once in a while last fall after her then-boyfriend Tyler Garrison—from Minnesota—broke up with her. After they broke up, she got closer and closer to me.

I can smash with chicks and still like boys.

Boys will eventually grow up and make sense, I guess.

I, like, love Amy, and she loves me, but it's not like that. Right now we're just good for each other. She looks after me, and I look after her, and sometimes we fool around. Other times we like to find a guy who thinks he knows it all at a club like Chocolate and take him to our apartment and get wetter than a slip-and-slide, which is really why our place is such a mess right now. And then he'll leave and it'll be just me and Amy again.

"Eey leeke zee Chineze wuhmahn," Borgen said when we got to our apartment. He was more plastered than a pissant. Some accents are sexy: a drunk Russian speaking English is not.

"I'm not Chinese," I said, which is definitely true. I'm from Johnston County, North Carolina, a peach blonde, DD cup, a few sun freckles on my cheeks. Amy says I'm super healthy thick in my thighs.

"I'm not Chinese either," Amy said then. We were in the living room and Amy held a bottle of Jägermeister.

"Eey wahnt zee Amy-Amy, boom-boom," Borgen said. He started to get naked right in the living room, but we pulled him to Amy's bedroom first.

A guy like Borgen would have never been my choice

for a one-night whatever. It was all Amy's idea. At Chocolate, she pulled me to a corner and said, "He's a gold medalist, Aim." She calls me Aim sometimes. "Hello, bucket list."

"Not my type or my list."

"Come on. I'm sure it'll be unforgettable. I dare you, bitch."

Men always think they have to *be* strong, so they overdo everything: how they move, think, fuck. Borgen had whiskey-dick. He couldn't get it up. Amy tried. I tried. He passed out on her floor.

That's when I took it.

After that, Amy and I got naked and fooled around and then ate ramen noodles because we were so hungry. It was three in the morning then.

At first, when Borgen woke, he had no idea where he was. When he saw us on the bed, he was all excited, like he'd won a second gold medal. He asked Amy how he was with his *sexy*. I faked like I was still sleeping.

"Your what?" I heard Amy say.

"*Eey mahde zee nice sexy, no?*" he said.

Amy played along. She said all the *sexy* made her really, really tired.

Then Borgen realized he wasn't wearing his medal. He went on and on about his Hammer Throw gold medal, replaying his every moment like he'd created the Heavens and the Earth. "*Vair eez eet?*"

"You don't remember?" I finally said, fake waking, not leaving the bed.

"*Eey rrmember nahzing. Vhut hahpened?*" His neck was heaving.

"You gave the taxi driver your medal," I said.

He stuttered out: "*Zattt eez aaah nnnot aaah true.*" I finally wanted to laugh.

We painted his memory for him, me and Amy:

Amy's purse was stolen at Chocolate, you said you'd take us home, we found a cab, when we reached here, you didn't have money, the taxi driver said he would call the police if we didn't pay, you said you'd heard Chinese jail *vaz zoo bahd-bahd,* you gave him your gold medal and said, *Eey vill vin zee new one.* We made the *sexy,* all three of us, here in Amy's bed, it's a mess and hot, you said you wanted to sleep on the floor, you have to get back to your team before your flight leaves this morning for Moscow.

"*No, no, my medahl!*"

Whatevs.

"*Eey no bee-leeve deez.*"

You should leave.

Now.

Don't you remember, Borgen Kuznetsov from Goon Squad, Russia?

He left frantically to find the taxi driver.

Amy said she could *almost* check "fuck an Olympic athlete" off her bucket list.

"Technically, *we* still won the gold," I said.

She smirked and said she needed sleep. That's when she closed up.

To keep Amy, I might have to get a puppy one day.

Or train for a marathon?

A bucket list is for lovers.

She'll wake soon.

Maybe I should shave now.

"CHOSEN"

Travis, your cousin, showed you how to masturbate.

You were both ten. No one was at home. It was February and rainy. Travis pulled the curtains closed in the TV room and sat next to you on the couch. He took out two *XXL* magazines from his book bag.

"Where'd you get those?" you said.

"The barbershop."

"Tiko's?"

"He said I could have them." Travis took one and flipped to the Eye Candy section. "Here," he said and tossed you the second magazine. "Girls are at the back."

Page 67: Tanesha Turner. Caramel skin. Long, black, wavy-at-the-tips, white-girl hair. Twenty years old, 5'4", 125 pounds, body firm with the perfect amount of pudgy. Her ass, round as a peach, devoured a pink thong. She was on a couch, a pillow wedged at her crotch, her hands cupping her breasts.

Travis slid down his basketball shorts. You noticed he

had hair growing down there already. His penis was darker and bigger than yours. He spat in his palm.

"What are you doing?" you said.

"Whatcha mean, Zeke?"

You looked at the magazine. You weren't sure what to feel or do, so you read: *The Video Vixen of the Year Interview.*

XXL: What was it like being in Nelly's "Hot in Herre" video?

You looked again at your cousin. He was massaging himself with his wet hand.

TT: It was amazing. I mean, to be in the scenes with Nelly—some y'all won't see in the video—was real hot and steamy.

XXL: Is there footage of that?

TT: Nice try, but I won't kiss and tell.

XXL: You got to give us a little something, Tanesha. How do you like—

TT: Slow. And gentle. I don't like a man to hurry.

You spat on your hand then and slid down your shorts.

Middle school was easy. You and Travis went to Lindbergh in the heart of the East Side. Long Beach: where the ocean waves just tickle the shore. You won the school-wide reading contest in grades six and seven. You'd read everything you could: *Harry Potter*, the *Hardy Boys*, anything by Walter Dean Myers, you even finished some of the books on the high school reading list.

In the beginning of eighth grade, Travis brought a gun to school and got expelled. It was a Glock 9mm. Not loaded. No bullets in his book bag or in his possession. The girl sitting next to him—Regina Smith, the girl who wore a new weave every other week—saw it and screamed. Travis zipped his book bag closed and ran out of the class.

Your mom took you out of Lindbergh. "You're going to St. Anthony's," she said.

You had just come inside from shooting hoops at the park. "What about Travis?" you said.

She stopped chopping the onions for the meatloaf. Her eyes were wet. "I don't care if y'all cousins, you're not getting caught up in all this gang nonsense," she said.

"Why, Mama—"

"Ezekiel James," she said, "the subject is closed."

Travis told you later he wasn't going to shoot anybody. A month after the incident, you went to see him after church on a Sunday. Your mom was in the living room with your Aunt Gale, crying. You remember her always crying back then like she was on the edge of something. You and Travis went to his room.

"Why'd you even have a gun anyway?" you said.

"I was just holding it for somebody," Travis said.

"Where'd you get it?"

Travis didn't say anything.

You told him about St. Anthony's.

"Oh, yeah," Travis said, "That's cool. Wanna play Madden?"

By grade eleven, your GPA was so high you were getting more college letters about academics than about basketball. Stanford, Harvard, Brown, Columbia, MIT. You were the St. Anthony Saint's salutatorian. You built a voice-operated robot named BIRTH.A that won an award at the state competition.

By that time, your cousin Travis was in the Orange County Juvenile penitentiary, serving time for Robbery and Assault. You begged your Granny to go with you to visit him, but she said, "Ezekiel, what makes you think I want to see my grandson in there like that?"

When you did visit, you asked Travis what happened.

"Zeke," he said, "it won't even like that, man. You know how the police is."

You nodded like you knew and played dominoes until the visit was over and Travis went back to his cell.

You were still a virgin until your senior year and one night at a house party this white girl named Melissa, who was the school soccer star, asked why you didn't have a girlfriend.

"Maybe I do," you said.

She squinted her white-girl blue eyes at you. "You're lying. I can tell."

You just grinned.

"Maybe you don't even like girls."

You were drunk—or getting there. "Maybe I don't," you said, and you're not sure why you said it, or even what it meant, but you knew you could never really mean it. Not being from the East Side. Melissa came closer to you then and pressed her white-girl body up on you and you two kissed and you faked like you were into it, but really robots excited you more.

St. Anthony's prepared you for your preppy east coast Ivy League life, but you were surprised at the rain and white people. They were both heavy and tiresome, but the rain felt real. Classes were easy. By your sophomore year, it was all a shit show. You fucked guys and girls, sometimes at the same time. It didn't matter. You fucked guys hard and girls soft. You took your time with the girls. You thought about how Tanesha Turner wanted it slow and gentle, so you were always soft with the girls.

Back home, Travis was finally getting out of juvy. He had his "Leaving Out" party, and your mom called and told you all about it. There was a cake. A few security guards and one of the administrators made an appearance. Travis had earned his GED and a barber certificate. Your mom posted a glossy photograph on Facebook of her and Travis, the painted seascape on the cement wall behind them inside the visiting center. Travis, head shaved with a beard, crisp royal blue button-up shirt with the dark blue jump pants and the California Department of Corrections logo, stood next to your mom and smiled. The caption read: *God Bless my nephew Travis. He'll be home next week. Thank you, Jesus!* Travis's mother, your Aunt Gale, was on the streets again, turning tricks for dope.

You still played ball and fucked around with robots, but you majored in Law and Psychology. Your senior year you thought you were in love with a Mexican man named Javier. He was easy and gorgeous. He was into photography and bondage. He'd read Pablo Neruda poems to you in Spanish when you lay naked on his squeaky mattress in his Washington Heights apartment.

"I've never been with a black man before," he said.

"And?"

"My family," he said, "Too much machismo. They'd never get us."

You thought about Travis. If you couldn't tell Travis, you might as well keep it a secret to everyone. You thought maybe it wasn't even true. You actually did like girls. You told Javier about Travis. He shook his head and said it was so *triste*.

"He'll stay out," you said.

"Think about how tough it's going to be for him. To try to find a job as a felon."

"Not Travis," you said. "He's too confident. Too smart."

"That might not be enough, *cariño*."

You thought for a moment. You wanted to tell Javier to shut the fuck up and just keep reading Neruda, but you waited.

You dressed. Before you left, you said, "Sometimes the things you do, don't tell the world who you really are."

Two years later, you're breathing rarefied air at Stanford Law School. You try not to think about home because you feel like you left everyone there on the East Side even though they tell you how proud of you they are. If you slow down, you'll sigh inside like a worn-out trumpet, so you don't slow down.

You date a woman who's ten years older than you: Naomi. She has a past that's so similar to yours, you don't need to talk about it. It's liberating not to have to have a past. She's already practicing law, working as a public defender.

Everything is physical between you and Naomi. Work, food, talking, fucking. You fuck her hard because there's no other way she wants it. You barely talk after. You just breathe and try not to think.

"I'm so tired of seeing young brothas go to jail and not getting out, Zeke," she said one day after work. You were two whiskeys in. She held a gin and tonic. "I need to be on the other side," she said. "Get paid for actually winning something instead of getting paid to lose." She even talked about going to Africa to see The Motherland and never coming back.

"You know that's not you," you said. "As fucked up as it is, America *is* our motherland."

You stay focused. Keep your head down and do work. Do right. That's what your mother taught you. *Especially when no one's looking,* she said. That's integrity. Do right all the time. Even if you're the only East Sider in every stuffy Stanford law school classroom and your classmates look to you to answer questions about Affirmative Action and soul food and how to do the Wobble.

You think about Travis. You picture him, still in Long Beach. Still on the East Side. He's probably still selling dope. Gang banging. Because what else would he be doing. He's got a ten-month-old girl named Ariella. His baby-mama is Mexican. He always had a thing for tamales and Latinas. There was danger in it too, dating one of them Northside Longos motherfucker's sisters or cousins. Travis could pull it off. He was smooth like that.

You study every day, getting ready to sit for the bar exam, but then your mother calls and says your Granny fell again.

"It's bad this time, Zeke," she says.

"What do you mean bad?"

Your mother is quiet for a few beats. "I'm going to find your Aunt Gale tomorrow. Take her up to see Mama."

You know what that means. You tell your mother you'll be home tomorrow.

Travis gets you at LAX.

You pop palms. One. Two. Three. Lock thumbs. Hands rise high, spread like bird's wings. Fingers wave and fall.

"Cuzzo," he says.

"Cuzzo."

You haven't talked in a while, but you don't have to talk like that. More is said during the pauses anyway. At the hospital, Travis doesn't even look at his mother. You know he judges her in a way you'll never understand. You make nice with Aunt Gale, because, you think, maybe this time she'll get clean.

Granny doesn't make it through the night. Travis punches his fist through a glass door window at the hospital. He was yelling at a doctor, telling him it was his fault his grandmama died. You hold Travis back, even when he says, "Man, don't touch me like that. You don't know me."

At the funeral Travis tells the story about when you and him got in trouble. "Back when we was younger," he says, "me and Zeke was up at King's Park, and I bet Zeke I could hit this beehive hanging up high in the tree with a rock. Back then we wasn't nothing but elbows and ashy kneecaps." He looks at you then. You're sitting between your Mom and his. You look up at him and try to hold it all together. "You remember that, Zeke?" he says.

You nod yes. The beehive. The memory comes rushing back.

It was no more than ten feet high and looked like a tense scrotum. You sealed the bet with a firm shake. On the first try, Travis slung the rock, like he was Doc Gooden, and it bopped the middle of the beehive. You watched him strut around yelling and bragging until the bees swarmed. You both thwacked at them. Travis's wrist and arm swelled and you ran together through the woods and back along the path and out of the park and kept running after the bees were gone.

"On the way to Granny's, we found a twenty-dollar bill," Travis says, "and tried to buy out the corner store."

Everyone laughs.

"We came in, like, two hours late with Cheetos smeared everywhere. My belly ached so bad, but Granny was there in the living room waiting. She had her big white Bible opened on the table."

Everyone gets giddy then. Says either *uh-oh* or lets the word *Lord* fall out of their mouth like a slinky. Not the big white Bible. That was Granny's Granny's Bible. The letters on the cover shine gold and when it's opened, the pages, thin and silky, feel weightless compared to the heaviness of when it's closed. It's bookmarked with bills, letters, envelopes of cash money, church service bulletins and announcements, pictures, and each of her children's and grandchildren's birth certificates. Everyone who knows your Granny, knows that Bible. She was singing to herself when you and Travis came strolling in. She asked where you two were, and you and Travis lied and kept lying and then she told you to sit on the couch and she told you the story of the serpent and how God knows when you're lying. How God knows everybody's heart.

"Granny had that way with everyone in the world she met," Travis says. "It's like God was always right there in her ear, telling us exactly what we needed to hear. At just the right time too, you feel me?" You hear *Amen* and *Hallelujah* and *Praise Jesus*.

As Travis steps down, you hug each other and say, "Love you, man," almost in unison.

The whole neighborhood shows up at the "Going Home" party.

"This ain't no pity-party," your Mom tells everyone. "This is a celebration. Mama is going to be with God."

You eat and drink. And drink. Late night, on the porch, you see Regina Smith.

"So you a lawyer now, huh, Zeke?" she says.

It's dark. You can't see her very well, but you can feel her smiling. "Will be soon," you say.

"You got you a girlfriend, Mr. Standford man?"

She says it like that—Standford, not Stanford—but you don't correct her, because, you think, who gives a fuck anyway. "Maybe," you say.

Later, you go to her house. She's got kids. They're asleep somewhere down the hallway. You think about Naomi, but you tell yourself she'd understand. This isn't about cheating. You're not a cheater. It's about you. You need to hold onto something before you let it go. You know you won't have too many more nights on the East Side. You have to say goodbye. Once you start making money, you'll buy your Mom a house in the valley like she's always wanted. The East Side will become the place where you grew up. The place you'll tell people *that made you.*

Regina plays Jodeci and gets naked faster than Naomi and Javier and even white-girl Melissa who wanted to do it all the time. Regina's got a scar on her stomach that you assume is from a C-section. You slide in her easily and take your time swimming in her thighs. You do it once and then again. She brings you lemonade and a plate of leftovers. You fall asleep to candlelight and the smell of alcohol on Regina's breath.

Your cell phone rings and you ignore it, but it rings again and again until you finally look. It's Travis.

"What, man?" you say. "You know what time it is?"

"Yo, Zeke, I need your help. You ain't at the house?"

"No."

"Where you at? I'm a come get you."

"I'm at Regina's."

He laughs. "Damn, son," he says, "I know what you've been up to."

"Man," you say, "it's not even like—"

"I'll be there in ten minutes. Meet me on the street."

"Okay," you say and immediately regret it. You weigh it all. No, you tell yourself, Travis wouldn't put me in the middle of something illegal. Something that would get me caught up. You know what can happen at 3 a.m. on the East Side. You and Travis have never had that discussion, but you know he knows there's a line drawn between worlds. You know he knows even though you're kin, you're really just a visitor. Have always been, like you were somehow chosen.

You leave without Regina waking.

The SoCal night air is breezy. A little chilly.

Travis pulls up in a black BMW. It's not his car or the car he picked you up in at LAX. "Get in," he says, "let's go."

You get in.

He drives for a bit.

There's no one else on the street.

"Trav," you say, "what's up, man?"

"You all right, Cuzzo," he says. "I just need you to drive my car. You going to follow me to my house. Don't worry, man."

You nod, but think a million things.

Another five minutes and you're there. At the AM/PM on Pacific Coast Highway. Travis pulls in at tank number 5. 87 is $2.65 a gallon. He pulls the gas lever in the driver seat floorboard. "I'm a fill up." He hands you his car keys. "I'm parked there," he gestures behind. "All you gonna do is follow me home."

You nod and take the keys.

Travis gets out and walks to the pump.

You think to ask if he's all right, but you don't. You're drained. You smell like sex. You feel sweaty in your stained suit. You have a flight tomorrow evening back to Stanford. You told your Mom you would've stayed longer, but you know Granny would want you to pass that bar exam and get on with it. *Just stay focused,* Granny always said. *Keep your head down and just stay focused.* You get in Travis's car and turn the ignition, crack the windows.

Travis is there in front of you, pumping gas. You can't see his face, but his body looks stiff, stressed. The morning-night neon of the AM/PM logo stares at a glowing Popeyes across the street. You take out your phone and text Naomi: *Be back tomorrow night.* You know she's sleeping, but she'll be up soon. She's an early riser. You'll text her your flight details later. You figure you'll go for drinks and order in—

Bop Bop.

It happens so fast.

Bop.

You fumble the phone. It falls in your lap. You duck low, across the middle console.

Bop Bop.

Bop Bop.

You wait.

Tires screech and peel out. It might be one car. Might

be two.

You take inventory. You're breathing, not bleeding. Slowly, you rise. Look.

The gas pump is still connected to the black BMW.

Travis is on the ground.

You think twice about getting out, but do it anyway. It's Travis.

You run to him.

His blood there on the pavement looks like it might swallow his body.

"Travis," you hear yourself say, "Travis, get up!"

You hear yourself because you are outside of yourself. It's like you're watching every moment from somewhere above. You remember reading about this in Psychology. You wrote a paper about it, didn't you? You've written a paper about just about everything.

Travis doesn't move. He's on his back. His chest is riddled with entry wounds. His chest is smoking, but he can't be dead.

Not Travis.

"Cuzzo," you hear yourself say louder. "Get up."

You hear sirens swarming from every direction.

"Trav," you say, "police coming, man."

You look inside the gas station. The clerk is on the phone, peeking through the window. His mouth is moving like he's screaming.

"Travis!" you hear yourself yell. You've never yelled

anything louder.

You can smell the Popeyes fried chicken just a few hundred feet away, but you've always preferred Louisiana up the street, by the park with the beehive.

That beehive: the rocks, the line in the dirt, the thwack when the feldspar hit the tree and the bees swarmed and you ran and Travis ran.

The East Side!

That's where it all began. You look at Travis. This is where it will end. You know you have to run for your life now, not his.

"NORMAL EARL"

Grandpa started losing his mind the summer the cicadas drove everyone crazy in Carroll County. I was ten. It was the same year Dad killed Joe Pesci our rooster. Joe Pesci was spotted black and white and had blue tail feathers and his wattle hung almost to his stomach. Dad loved all those Italian mobster movies and he said Joe Pesci was the meanest dude. He was a meaner rooster. One time, Joe Pesci pecked the head off one of our hens. I don't remember her name, but she was one of the pretty, all-white ones. He got on top of that hen and started pecking at her like he was drunk or crazy. The hen cackled *cluckaaawk cluckaaawk* over and over and we tried to scare Joe Pesci away but it was too late.

"Son," Grandpa said. He called everybody he cared about son. "That rooster is meaner than hell." Grandpa got worked up about Joe Pesci, red mustangs, and his homemade wine.

Dad killed Joe Pesci a few weeks after the hen. It was

an accident. We were all on the back porch. It was barely dusk and everything was warm. The lightning bugs were out, but the cicadas were so loud I thought the earth might explode. All of a sudden Joe Pesci ran through the back yard like he was up to something.

Grandpa said, "Look at that that goddamn rooster go," and laughed.

We all laughed and then Dad finished the last swallow from his Coca-Cola bottle and hurled it high and fast. The bottle bopped Joe Pesci on the head and he fell over dead right there in the yard. I asked Dad if we'd eat him, but Grandpa said, "Son, it'd take at least two settings to chew through that devil rooster's thigh meat."

Whenever I tell Dr. Judy stories about Grandpa, she always says the same thing: "That's lovely, Earl, and what do your memories about your grandfather mean to you today?"

I always sigh like I'm a dying squirrel and say the same thing, which is, "I don't know, I guess."

Her office is painted puke green and, last week, as I was leaning back in her leather psychiatrist's chair, I was getting nauseous looking at all that green and I asked her why she chose that color.

She looked around the room, confused. "I was thinking it was more like pea green."

"I know puke when I see it," I said. "I guess you like it and that's what counts." I'm a nurse. Or was.

She asked if I thought it was going to snow.

There's one window in Judy's office on the second floor. I have to turn my head just slightly to the left to see it. Outside, the sun was breathless, stuck behind streaks of gray clouds layering the sky. "I don't know," I said.

"Crazy to think we'll get snow in late March in Raleigh, isn't it?"

"I don't know." I turned my head from the window then. We all moved to Raleigh the summer I turned a teenager, right after Grandpa died and Dad didn't want anything to do with the farm.

"What do you want to talk about today, Earl?"

I shrugged. "Just whatever, I guess."

"Who were you in high school?"

"Who what?"

"In high school. What kind of kid were you? Sports? Classes? Did you take a foreign language?"

Judy does this a lot. Picks and pokes. Sometimes I wish she'd just jump on me with a scalpel and rib shears. Go on and get it over with already.

"I took Latin," I said.

"Latin?" I could hear her scribbling on her notepad. "Why Latin?"

"I thought it'd be cool to speak a language no one spoke any more. Plus, I wanted to be a doctor."

"Do you remember your teachers?"

Jesus, I thought. High school was twenty years ago.

There was fat Mr. Garner. He taught Physics. I played baseball. Listened to Nirvana and Wu-Tang Clan. "This girl Nicole and I used to write notes back and forth in History class."

"What kind of notes?"

"All sex notes," I said. It was true. "About how she wanted it and how she let her boyfriend, who was much older than her and not in high school or college, tie her up in different ways. She started it."

"And what did you write to her?"

"I can't remember. I just remember that was way more interesting than History."

It was quiet for a minute. Judy does this too, sometimes. Just lets everything linger. Then, I said: "My English teacher told us a story about how her dogs were stolen. She said she had one dog—I can't remember what type—and that dog was stolen right from her yard. She went and got another dog and then that dog was stolen too. We all laughed at her behind her back."

"Why would your English teacher tell you this in class?"

"I have no idea. I think we were reading *Gatsby*. I used to smoke pot before class in the back seat of Jeff Limbo's Jeep Wrangler. I think that's why her dog story was so funny."

"That is a funny story."

"I think her name was Ms. Baker," I said, looking up at the ceiling. "Yeah, Ms. Baker. She was this short, black lady who always wore wool. Her favorite thing to say to us was, 'The only thing you have to do is pay taxes and die.'"

"Your high school English teacher sounds like a character. I imagine she was saying that in response to a student asking, *Do we have to?*"

I paused. Dr. Judy always tries to know everything.

"Never mind, Earl," she finally said. "I'm getting us off track. Those are all memories you have, but I want to hear you talk more about you."

"What do you mean?"

"Well," she said, flipping through pages of her notepad. "You've talked about your family, and I can picture moments from your life as you've described them, but why do you think you've become the person you are today. What do you think has brought you here, to this point in your life?"

I wanted to say, "You mean for me to want to jerk off in public?" but I didn't. It all came to a head, and I say that both facetiously and not, when I was caught masturbating at the Two-Dollar Cinema on Blue Ridge Road one evening about a month ago. I was by myself. It was 1:30 in the afternoon on a Tuesday. Who goes to the movie theater at 1:30 on a Tuesday afternoon? It was a romantic comedy with Reese Witherspoon. I have a thing for Reese Witherspoon. I didn't know indecent exposure carried a felony charge and I didn't know there was a teenage girl with her mom in the theater that day either. Why wasn't she in school, huh, mom, I wanted to say when I watched them fade away in the distance as the police car left the parking lot. I'm not a pedophile, but no one except for Judy listens about that anymore. It was my first offense. I lost my job and was mandated by the court to see a shrink three times a week.

"I was a good student. A really good student," I told Judy. I was lying. "I played soccer and baseball."

"Let's project into that a bit, Earl. How were you good? What made you a good student? Why did you play soccer?"

"Sorry, Dr. Judy, but I'm not sure I understand what you mean." I call her Dr. Judy when I think she is talking gobble-dee-goop. "All that was a long time ago. Why does anybody do anything anyway? How about: I liked to feel my lungs fill with air when I ran. I liked to learn and to read." That last part was true. I did read a lot. "Isn't that normal?"

"Everything's normal and not normal," she said. "It depends on how the individual defines it. What are the boundaries, what are the rules, what's non-negotiable, and what's not."

It started to sound a lot like the *mindfulness* crap Dr. Judy had been trying to sell me. Mindfulness had been everywhere at work lately too. At the hospital. "Hmmm," I said. "I guess, Dr. Judy, then, what I am isn't normal."

It's a small office. You can feel everything inside there.

I could feel her shaking her head no, trying to save me. "We're all *not* normal, Earl."

All goble-dee-goop. "Even you?" I said.

"Even me." She was lying, and I started to hate myself again. "Did you have any girlfriends in high school or in college?"

We'd been over my recent love life already, which was bare. "I did," I said. "We dated for two years in high school. She was a year older."

"What was that like?"

"It was high school. Aren't all high school relationships the same?"

"How so?"

"All awkward and angst-y."

"Maybe. I married my high school sweetheart."

Judy hadn't really revealed much of herself to me. "Of course you did," I wanted to say, but instead I said, "Is that normal?"

She laughed at this. "Probably not," she said. "Why did you and—what was her name?"

"Jennifer."

"What is the story of Earl and Jennifer in high school?"

I laughed at this. I told her about how we met, which was at a football game. We'd been eyeing each other for several weeks. It was all negotiations back then. You talked to your friend to talk to one of her friends to set up an activity or something that usually involved the mall. The whole group is there, at the mall, or wherever, until it dissipates and it's just you and her. That's how it was at the football game. It was everyone and then me and Jennifer at the snack bar. I don't know what all we said to each other. You just sort of slide into dating and then you're there. I told Judy all of this.

"That's adorable," she said. I imagined she had a similar story about her husband. "Why'd you break up?"

"You're not going to ask if she was my first."

"Okay," she said, "Was she your first?"

"No," I said, firm and hard. She didn't ask who was.

"I care more about how your relationships begin and end," she said.

I hadn't heard Judy reveal her game plan like that to me before. She was up to something.

"Oh," I said, "Well, I should tell you something then."

She didn't say anything. She was waiting.

"Whenever Jennifer got real drunk and passed out, I'd take pictures of her."

"Pictures? What kind of pictures?"

"The kind of pictures Nicole drew in History class."

"Really?"

"Yes."

"Did you ever—"

"No," I said. I knew Judy was going to ask if I played with Jennifer when she was passed out drunk. I'm not like that. "Never. She knew actually."

"You told her?"

"She caught me one night."

"She caught you?"

Judy does this all the time. Repeats what I say, like I'm talking to a mirror. "Yes, she caught me."

"What did she say."

"She didn't care. She just said I better not do anything with them."

"And did you?"

"No," I said. I was telling the truth. Sort of.

"Never?"

"No. They were just for me." The truth was, I'd look at them at home in bed or in the blue bathroom and masturbate.

Judy was scribbling things on her notepad, judging me. After a while, she said, "So, why did you two break up?"

"Ha!" I said. "This is the best high school break-up story ever."

"I'll be the judge of that."

I laughed at this. Judy is pretty funny when I think about it. Jennifer is still in Raleigh. I've found her on Facebook. She has kids and a dorky-looking husband. They sell real estate together, which is perfect. Just perfect.

"My high school had these epic pep rallies. Everyone got really into it. Jennifer was a cheerleader and on the night before the big Senior-Sophomore/Junior-Freshman pep rally, after Jennifer and all her senior girlfriends finished decorating the halls with posters and signs, my buddy and I broke into the school and tore it all down."

"What do you mean?"

"I mean we ripped the posters and streamers from the walls. All the things that said the seniors were the best and all that. We tore it down."

It took Judy so long to respond I thought she was writing an essay about me. She finally said: "That doesn't seem like a nice thing to do."

"I know. It was awful."

"You got caught again, didn't you?"

"That's my M.O., isn't it? Getting caught red-handed."

There was a pause again, and I wanted more than anything for Dr. Judy to say, *Or with your pants down*, because that would have been funny and I'd stop hating myself for a second or two in that puke green room. She was scribbling shit again on her notepad.

"Well," she finally said, "What did Jennifer say?"

"She said she'd been cheating on me anyway with this kid who had a really bad stutter, but everyone was still afraid of him for some reason. I think he was a model or something for Abercrombie."

Judy stood then and turned on the lamp right by the window. It was getting darker outside. After she sat back down, she said: "Let's take this a bit further, Earl."

I shrugged. "Okay."

"I want to ask you about your father."

"My father?"

"Yes, your father."

I nodded.

"Did he ever touch you?"

"Dad?"

She said that most sex addicts, not all but most, had some traumatic or sexual abuse experiences as children that could have caused an inability later in life to control sexual urges and impulses.

"No," I said.

"You don't recall ever in your childhood—maybe back on the farm—something happening that . . . didn't feel right?"

Why does everything have to have an explanation. There are worse things in the world than being like me. How about, This is what God gave me, Dr. Judy? How about that? "No," I said. "Dad, Mama, Grandpa. Nothing. It's only all good memories."

She seemed satisfied with that and scribbled some more. "Tell me about one of your recent moments."

"You want me to tell you about Reese Witherspoon again?"

"No, no, not that. I'm sure, Earl, there have been other moments. Other moments that led you to the movie theater."

She was trying to get at how long I'd been doing what I'd been doing. How long I'd been starving for flesh. I haven't told my parents about any of it. They're old and already moved back to Carroll County, back to the country. They'd just worry, and nobody wants their parents to worry.

"I paid for sex once when I was in college," I said. "I drove to the Mustang Ranch in Zebulon and asked one of the strippers how much it'd cost for her to do more than a lap dance." I knew then that wouldn't be enough. Judy was scribbling. I'm not sure if there's an exact moment when it all crosses over. Are we all just hovering at some invisible threshold? Does it grow and evolve until it consumes you? I didn't say all that though. "Porn only went so far," I told Judy. I'd subscribed to the most erotic online sites, but the videos didn't feel real. I paid for and joined live-streaming chat rooms. Each girl was almost always dressed and posturing in the same way: wearing bra and panties, lying on her bed with the keyboard at her fingertips, grinning into the computer screen back at me. The slight video delay aroused me even more, elongating the anticipation of it all. I'd type what I wanted to see her do—whoever she was—and she'd penetrate herself with whatever toy she had or maybe it was just her hand, and I did the same, pleasuring myself. I was on several sites at a time. Click, click, click. I had a few aliases. *NurseIsThor. CallmeEarl. LiptonService.* I'd spend hours reading personal ads on Backpage.com: Women Seeking Men and Men Seeking Women, sometimes Men Seeking Men. Just to see all the flesh, but it was never enough.

I kept jerking off to this one young, black girl from Durham named Lottice who'd written in her Women Seeking Men ad on Backpage that she was looking for a white man who would "cum to her every want and need." Her phone number was there with the ad and one night I decided to text her. She texted back with an address. I drove to Durham, to a Motel 6, and went to room 203, like her text message directed. I knocked. She opened the door. I could see the rug and the cheap bed that had been the subtle backdrop to the teasing pictures she'd uploaded online.

I told Judy that Lottice looked a lot younger in person, but I skipped telling about all the sex we had in her motel room. That's not what she really wanted to hear about anyway, I know.

"How did you feel after your . . . "

"Sport fucking."

Judy cleared her throat then. "Is that what you call it?" I shouldn't have said it like that. It's not Dr. Judy's fault.

"Lottice fell asleep and I was lying on the bed naked and smeared with KY jelly. I thought about cutting off my penis right there in the Motel 6. If I didn't have a penis, would I still be a nympho? Wouldn't it just all be easier?"

I stopped talking then for a moment. The room was colder and I could feel Judy trying to be quiet, letting it all linger. It was like she was cutting out my insides. "I almost fell asleep, but then I heard a baby crying in the bathroom."

"A baby?"

I nodded. "Lottice wasn't moving. I got up from the bed." I'd tried to put this part out of my mind. "It was just a plain, white Motel 6 bathroom, but Lottice had all her make-up and brushes and combs and girly products on the counter. I pulled the shower curtain, and there was a small, wooden crib rocking a baby."

I think I scared Dr. Judy. She wasn't expecting that. This story wasn't normal at all. "What did you do?" she said.

"At first, I thought it was a sign from God."

"A sign of what?"

"I don't know. Hope, maybe. I mean, Lottice, the slut, is a mother. I'm way worse than Lottice, but why can't I be a father too? I'm not all bad. Why can't I have a child one day and raise him so he won't be anything like me."

There was a pause. Judy was waiting for more.

"I picked it up and held it until Lottice woke up. For a moment, we were there in the bathroom together, I was cuddling the baby and Lottice was by my side. Sort of like a mother and father. Sort of like a family."

Judy was scribbling like she was having an orgasm. "What happened next?"

"Lottice gave me a look and took the baby from my arms. I got dressed and left." I was done.

After a while, Judy lightened the mood. She went back to asking me about Grandpa. That's how it all starts and ends with Dr. Judy: Grandpa. I think that's her game plan with everybody.

"Time's almost up for today," she finally said. "But, Earl, I need to know. Have you ever thought about—"

I sat up then and interrupted Judge Judy. "Suicide?" I said. I turned and looked at her. Judy's funny, but she's too nice. I bet she takes her work home with her. She'll probably tell her husband about Earl Lipton and his sex addiction. "It's never crossed my mind." I was lying.

Our session was over then. Outside, it was somewhere between sleeting and snowing. I drove around town until I found a Starbucks. Instead of going through the drive-through like I usually do, I parked and walked inside. There were people there, sipping lattes and mochas and talking. I bought a tall black coffee and went back to my truck.

If I did kill myself, I'd leave the truck engine running in the garage and sit naked and more lubed than a racecar. I'd play "Song of the South" over and over, because Grandpa loved Alabama.

If I had a son, I'd name him Shelton or Earl Junior. I'd watch him catch lightning bugs with a Mason jar, like Dad and Grandpa did with me. He'd ask me about the men in the family who came before me and him. I'd keep it simple. He'd be ten. That's when boys want to know everything. I'd tell him the truth. That some things can be explained in the world and some things can't be.

I'd tell him that his granddaddy was a mechanic and could fix any car, but he smoked too many cigarettes.

"What's that mean?"

"It means cigarettes clogged his insides and he coughed himself to death."

"Did it hurt him?"

"Hurt me worse, son."

"Oh."

Shelton would have hair like mine, dusty brown and shaggy. He'd have my elongated second toe and bowlegs too.

"What about your daddy's daddy?" Shelton would say next. "What happened to him?"

I'd want Grandpa's tone then. Tall and strong and stoic. "Your great-grandfather," I'd say, "was a farmer."

"What'd he farm?"

"Cattle."

"Did you ever farm with him?"

"A little bit, I did."

"What happened to him?"

"Well, son," I'd say, taking my time, feeling the space between my son and me. "He had Alzheimer's."

He'd look around and then his eyes would wander back to mine and he'd say, "What's old-timers?"

I'd smile then and rub his hair. I'd kiss him on the forehead and tell him I loved him. Forever and ever. After all the cicadas were dead and gone. No matter what in the world he wanted to do or be. "Sometimes, son," I would start, and then I'd lean in a little more, making sure he could touch me and I could hold him. That would be enough. "Sometimes it's sunny and warm out and there's not a cloud in the sky, and then all of a sudden, clouds roll in and it rains and you have to postpone baseball practice. And then, after a while you have to cancel practice for good. Alzheimer's is kind of like that. When everything's cloudy all the time." I can see Shelton looking at me, like I'm his hero, like how I looked at Grandpa.

I sipped my tall black coffee, thinking about it all. The whole sky turned into snow then and pattering snowflakes whited the windshield and then whited all the rest of the windows, and I felt, finally, like it was all becoming a cocoon of white and maybe new again.

"SUBURBAN WHITE GIRL LOVE AFFAIR (OR STUBBORN LOVE)"

1.

At the Trinity Wellness Center in west Raleigh, Allison John is stretching Mr. McFerlot's hamstring on the therapy table and Mr. McFerlot says, "Did you hear about how them Muslim men up in that house were all tootie fruitie?"

Allison recalls the nightly news footage from the day before: a gang of I.C.E. officers surrounded an unsuspecting suburban home in Fuquay-Varina and, after breaching the front door with a battery ram, dragged out five brown men—all frail and bare-chested, clad only in their boxer shorts—and four women, each garbed in a black burka, tiny slivers of their eyes showing, holding onto four little children.

"Tootie fruitie?" Allison says. "Mr. McFerlot, where in the world did you hear something like that?"

"On the radio. Anything goes these days, don't it, baby doll?" He's the same age as Allison's father and has a similar good ol' boy charm.

Allison gives him a look.

He does have a gruesome injury. A truck driver, he fell asleep at the wheel and ran head-on into signage at an exit ramp. He is lucky he only suffered a broken leg. "Can't you just see it? One of them Jihadists wearing women's undergarments and leggings, prancing around with his AK-47."

She digs her thumb hard in his thigh.

"Don't get sassy on me, missy, haven't I been working hard today?"

"Play nice, Mr. McFerlot."

"Dang, just telling it like it is. Going to hell in a hand basket—this whole country—if you ask me."

She digs deeper and he reels and *ouch*es even more, then she lets go and says, "All right, you're ready to cool down."

She walks to retrieve the ice packs for the last part of his rehab therapy, and when she returns, he says, "I heard one of them went to Athens."

She thinks for a beat. "Really?"

"What I heard."

"I went to Athens," she says.

"I figured you went to Cary or Athens. You're a local gal, right?"

She exaggerates her "yes," like *yeeaas*. "Born Raleigh proud."

After Mr. McFerlot's session is over, Allison rushes to the lounge and rustles through the newspaper, but there are no close-ups or names, there's just the aerial, helicopter footage, same as the live news, like something out of some Hollywood action flick. She can't help but think about a fling she had in high school with a boy named Raed.

Allison and her husband Tommy have three kids. Elizabeth is four; Eric six; and TJ—Tommy Junior—nine. She has never told Tommy about Raed. It isn't like Tommy has told her about all of the women he's slept with, she doesn't believe that for one minute. Besides, she's told her "first" story so many times, about how she lost her virginity to Grayson Sanford, her high school sweetheart, she's almost forgotten that, no, Raed was actually her first. How did that happen anyway, she thinks, staring at the brown men in the photo being whisked away in the blacked-out SUVs. She hasn't thought about *that* in years.

When Allison gets home she cooks Hamburger Helper and throws together a salad that no one but her touches. Tommy has poker with "the boys," so she's on duty for the night with the kids. TJ is easy. He'd just as soon leave the dinner table and read. Eric and Elizabeth are a handful, but Allison manages to get them bathed and calm for bed even though every night, without fail, Elizabeth tiptoes into her and Tommy's bedroom to sleep with them at some point.

The next morning, Allison can't believe her eyes. The *News and Observer* front page reads: "Local Muslim Men

Arrested, Accused of Plotting Terrorist Attacks." The ringleader is a forty-something former U.S. Marine who fought the Russians in Afghanistan, was shot in battle and won a Purple Heart, returned to the U.S., converted to Islam, and lived a relatively quiet family life. David Mahoney, also known as "Saifullah," ran a drywall business and looks like an everyday American Joe: sandy-brown hair, evenly-trimmed goatee, brown eyes, slight and assured grin. The rest of the men are all American citizens, but they are brown and their mug shots look like they've been pulled from a forgotten cave. There are Omar Abulaye Yaghi, 21; Muhammad Hassan, 22; Anes El Hadj Sherifi, 45; Zakariya Aly, 32; and then, there he is: Raed Habib Aswad, 37.

Allison feels like she might puke. What were the chances? She lost her virginity to a Jihadist? Is that what he is? What he was? Feeling dizzy, she paces the kitchen. The coffee machine is gurgling. She looks outside. The grass is green, the summer sun rising. It'll be hot like every other summer day. She breathes, turning again to the newspaper. What were the chances? He is much thicker in the face than she remembers. Bearded and head closely shaven now, his once handsome hazel-blue eyes gazing ghost-like at the camera. She can't believe it.

On Mahoney, one neighbor states: "I saw the family about every day out walking their dog. They waved. We waved. They seemed like nice folks. Not the terrorist type one bit."

Another says: "Their kids played with our kids. It's crazy. You just don't know this day and age who your neighbors really are."

Allison gets stuck on the line: "If convicted, they could all face the death penalty."

She hears Tommy coming down the stairs. She folds and scoots the paper to the end of the kitchen island. "You look rough," she says when Tommy reaches the room. "You win last night?"

He leans on the kitchen island. "I never win."

She pours him coffee. "You were trying to win with me when you came home. Your drunk hands were everywhere."

"Like I said, I never win."

"Not with little Lizzy there in the bed with us. You know that."

It's a long Fourth of July weekend, so the kids are still in their rooms. Tommy turns his attention to the newspaper.

"Eggs and bacon all right?" Allison says, turning to busy herself.

"Mm-hmm. Jesus, my head hurts."

"We're still going to the lake house today, right? I texted Crystal we were."

"Says this one went to Athens. Ally, you see this?"

Not looking to Tommy, she says, "No. We only got

three eggs, maybe we just get Bojangles' on the way out."

"Fine. Ally, paper says he graduated '98. That's your class. Come here and look."

She sighs. "Let me see." She walks to Tommy. "Which one?"

He points. "Raed Habib Aswad. Did you know him?"

She looks closer. "Him? No, don't think so."

"Holy Habiby, he looks like a terrorist."

"You still smell like booze."

"Trump is right. We should build a wall."

"They're citizens, Tommy."

"You know what I mean. It's just all a little scary, isn't it?"

It is, she thinks. You could get shot at the mall or at church or learn that you lost your virginity to a Jihadist.

Allison's short and still fit. She was a soccer star in high school. Tommy, who played college football, is now just burly, wide, and jock-looking. When they embrace, it looks like his body could swallow her whole. He sells real estate and still eats like he works out each day. Allison's been warning him it's only a matter of time before his metabolism slows down.

"How does something like this happen here anyway?" he says.

She moves back into the kitchen, opening the refrigerator again. "I don't know, Tommy. Maybe we just all eat cereal."

"Never thought you'd hear about this here in North

Carolina, you know what I mean?"

A few minutes pass and Allison hears the soft pounding of feet along the upstairs floors. Tommy's still reading the paper. She looks at him. "Kids are up."

"Yeah," he says, "I can't wait to get out to the lake."

"Me too," Allison says, but really she's stuck on *How did that happen?*

2.

Twenty-plus years earlier, *that* started one summer at the Hootie & The Blowfish concert. Allison and Grayson had a bad fight and fast breakup. Allison had first-hand evidence that Grayson hooked up with another girl from a different school. A week before the concert at the Cary Towne Center mall, Allison slapped Grayson in the face and then kicked him in the crotch. Grayson grabbed and shoved her to the linoleum floor. Everyone saw it.

"He's an asshole, a cheater, and he's violent," Crystal Whitley, Allison's best friend, said. "You can do better than that."

The Varsity Boys' and Girls' Soccer team captains organized the concert outing. All the players went together. On the lawn of the Walnut Creek Amphitheatre, Allison drunkenly sang "Let Her Cry" at the top of her lungs. She thought the last line of the chorus, "Ah, let her be," was some kind of mantra or epiphany, maybe, about love. That night she made out with Raed, there on the lawn. She'd thought Raed was so cute. They had AP Spanish together. He was new to school, had a different accent and name.

"I'm from Persia," Raed had said in class.

Allison had no idea what that meant. "Wow," she had said.

After that kiss at Walnut Creek, they spent the next three weeks in Spanish class passing notes back and forth until Raed finally asked her out:

Dinner at Chili's and then a movie?

They held hands for what seemed like the whole night and on the way home Raed parked behind the Kmart on Western Boulevard and they made out, listening to more Hootie.

A few more weeks passed and Allison fell even harder for Raed. Plus, she had heard Grayson was dating some freshman girl now. It dawned on her that she was the last in her group of girlfriends to "do the deed," which is how Crystal talked about sex. Allison had thought Grayson would be the one. They had so much history and, well, she'd always thought they'd be together forever. But why couldn't it be me and Raed forever, she thought.

She was almost seventeen. They had done more than just make out, and she figured he was ready for something more than her jerking him off while he fingered her. One Friday morning in Spanish class, she told him to come over that night when she paged him *143.

"Okay," he said.

She didn't tell him what the night would be about. It was supposed to be on her terms, when she told him it was time. That's how it went with sex, Allison was sure. She imagined them lying naked on the couch—or in her bed—hugged up like a pretzel, post-coital. They'd fall asleep together and that would be perfect.

She didn't tell him her parents were out of town either. She paged him at 7:16 p.m. and waited. When the phone finally rang, she said, "Raed, is that you?"

"Hey."

"You're not on the way yet?"

"Now?"

"Raed! I told you this morning to come over as soon as I page you."

"I just got out of the shower."

She could hear him rustling around his bedroom she'd actually never seen. His parents had rules. *Good Grades* was a rule. *No girls in the house* was a rule. It wasn't that extreme. She had a few crazy Christian friends whose parents had similar rules about grades and the opposite sex. "Hurry," she said, "Tell your parents you have a big test to study for or something like that."

"I'll be there soon," he said.

She imagined his room was like Grayson's: messy and gross. Clothes, towels, and dirty, sweaty socks thrown everywhere. Raed was still cute though. So cute.

She got the TV room in the basement all ready. She brought down her favorite pink fleece blanket from her bedroom, the one with the frayed edges that smelled like the kiwi-strawberry Body Shop spray. She popped popcorn and set two Cokes on the coffee table. She rewound *Aladdin* in the VCR and played with the lamps so the room was light enough for Raed to put the condom on the right way, but dim enough so he wouldn't notice the pimple on her forehead she'd tried to cover with the concealer Crystal told her to try.

Back in her bedroom, she gazed at herself in the mirror the way she thought models gazed at the camera in those Abercrombie & Fitch advertisements, which was something like a sexy pout. She decided to wear her gray, loungy sweatpants and a blue, long-sleeved T-shirt that read "Athens High Conference Champs 1995-1996." In the back of her top dresser drawer, where she stuffed scarves and gloves, there was a box of three Ultra Thin LifeStyles condoms that Crystal had given her. She'd said that the thicker ones always hurt worse. Allison took the box from the drawer, thought for a moment to just take one, but then put all three in her sweatpants pocket.

By the time she got back downstairs to the basement and lit one of the scented Yankee candles her mother kept in the bathroom closet, she heard a soft tapping on the front door. She rushed upstairs. "Hey," she said, opening the screen door for Raed.

He was smiling. "Hey, sorry I'm—"

"No," she said. "It's perfect. Really." She took his hand.

Allison's parents weren't the hovering, overbearing type. As long as she did well in school, which she did, and stayed out of trouble, which she did, she was "left to her own devices and whatnot," which is how her father put it. At work, Allison's father had won a weekend getaway at a *she-she-foo-foo* bed and breakfast out on the Outer Banks. Allison said she had no interest in either of those. "Plus," Allison had said, "soccer practice. Conference tourney in just a month."

"Fine," her father had said. "Just behave."

Allison nodded, *Yes, Daddy.*

The dimness of the basement was just as Allison had imagined: perfect. She still held Raed's hand. "You want to watch *Aladdin?*" she said.

"*Aladdin?*" He looked around the room. "I mean, yeah, sure."

They sat on the couch. She took a handful of popcorn and pushed one of the Cokes closer to him.

"Thanks," he said. "When do your parents get home?"

"They're not here."

"Not here?"

"They're out of town for the weekend."

"Oh."

She took the remote, pushed play, and then slouched

even further next to him. "Your eyes are so . . . striking. You don't see eyes like yours every day."

"Your eyes are really pretty, too," he said.

On the screen, a man riding a camel through the desert was singing "Arabian Nights."

Allison looked at Raed again and pinched his arm. "Hey," she said.

"Hey."

They tongue kissed until Aladdin was running through the market with his monkey Abu and then they stretched out on the couch. Allison lay in front of Raed and handed him a pillow to prop his head so he could see the movie. She took his arm and hugged it in her bosom. They'd never lain like that before.

It was a while before she felt his hand slip to the upper seams of her panties. *Aladdin* was her favorite and she knew every line by heart. Just before Jafar turned into the giant cobra, she turned to face Raed. She kissed him once on the lips and started to lick and kiss his neck. She could smell the Polo Sport cologne he'd sprayed too much of.

For some reason, at that moment, she couldn't get Crystal's line "do the deed" out of her mind and even thought about other, way worse things she'd overheard boys say about sex. She recalled waiting for Grayson one day in the gymnasium lobby, right by the boys' locker rooms, back when things were good with him, and one boy said something about "when you getting up in them guts, Gray."

She felt Raed's hands get even more erratic and less romantic, so she stopped him. She took her time kissing him on his lips and looking into his eyes. "Hey," she said, pulling the condom wrappers from her sweatpants pocket.

"What's—"

Allison didn't know what to think. Why didn't he finish his sentence? Was he judging her? Would he say no?

"Now?" he finally said.

She kissed him again, thinking, *I wish he was more . . .* She didn't know what exactly, but she'd made the move that told him yes and like everything else in the world, there's a time to jump in already. At least that's what her daddy always told her.

In the dimness she got naked and he pulled his boxer shorts to his ankles. She made sure the pink fleece blanket was near and wrapped it over them as he got on top of her. She remembered her girlfriends talking about their first time, like it was something to hurry up and get done. He put on the condom. Crystal had said, It all gets easier after you do it a few times. It was all awkward jamming. Allison wished she had something to ease him into her.

"Is it okay now?" he finally said.

"Yes," she said in a whisper.

The deed was done before she knew it. Underneath the pink fleece blanket, she wrapped her arms around him tighter. They both turned their heads to the screen. When the credits started to run, she could feel he'd gone limp.

"It's so hot," he said. "Can we lose the blanket?"

"What's *that*," she said.

"What?"

"What's that oozing?"

He lifted himself up off the couch, like he'd been poked in the ribs. "Shit."

"What?"

"Holy fucking shit."

"What?"

"Shit. Fucking shit."

She looked.

"The condom broke," he said.

She thought, *Damn it, Crystal, you and your Ultra Thin condoms.*

"What if you're pregnant," Raed said, standing, then pacing.

There was no post-coital cuddling. She handed him a box of Kleenex to clean himself.

Allison said, "Relax. Come." She motioned for him to join her on the couch. "Come here. Let's lay again."

"I'm such an idiot."

She watched him look at the broken, goopy condom sitting in a nest of Kleenex on the coffee table. "You're not the only one."

"That's not what I mean." He was still standing.

"What *do you* mean, Raed?"

"You don't get it. My father would kill me. If you're pregnant, my life is—"

"I'm not pregnant. Do you even know what the chances are of that," she said, but she wasn't sure. She'd read recently in *Seventeen* how some girls had gotten pregnant doing a lot less. Something about pre-cum. She'd read too how "copious amounts" of raw and cooked papaya was the natural equivalent to the morning-after pill.

Sometime around ten, Allison walked Raed to the door. She paged him throughout the weekend, but when he called back, she noticed he was short. "Raed, what's wrong?"

"Nothing. It's nothing. I have to go."

The next week at school went about the same.

She had to put what she and Raed did somewhere in the universe other than her journal and the calendar hanging on her bedroom wall—she'd drawn a heart around the date—and, well, she had Crystal. Allison finally told her a few days before Homecoming.

"Well, damn," Crystal said, "you sure know how to pick them."

"I thought all guys wanted was sex."

"They do, but you should go on the pill. Keeps your period regular too."

In Spanish class that week, Raed finally passed Allison a note: *Did you take the P test?*

I'm not pregnant

U sure?

You're an asshole.

Allison didn't reach for any more notes from Raed and during halftime at Homecoming, she and Grayson finally started talking again.

3.

Allison and Tommy share a lakeside home at Kerr Lake with Crystal and her husband Danny. The house is big enough for both families and they share everything: the mortgage, lake fees, house repairs, secondary home taxes, and the boats. Crystal and Danny bought a pontoon. Allison and Tommy have an eighteen-foot motor boat.

It's only an hour and a half to Kerr Lake, so by two o'clock, Tommy is steering their motor boat, cruising the summer lake waters, while Allison and the kids are seated and sunscreened, laughing at the heat and the splashing water.

The cell phone reception at the lake is shoddy, so Allison keeps resending her text to Crystal:

Hey girl don't say anything about Raed haven't told Tommy yet

Allison isn't even sure if Crystal knows anything about the terrible Jihadists in Fuquay-Varina. They're driving from Atlanta and won't get in until the evening.

When the water clears of jet-skiers and jon boats, Tommy speeds up, ripping through the water. The kids yell giggling *aahs.* Allison wonders if Raed has thought of her. Did he even sign her yearbook? She can't remember. To be fair, she hadn't really thought of him.

There are hardly any waves at Kerr Lake. It's perfect for this type of carefree speeding. "Hang on," Allison says as Tommy cranks the motor boat even faster. She hugs Lizzy in her lap even harder and hears Tommy yell, *Yeah buddy!*

Over the next few nights, fireworks will be heard across the lake, building more and more until Tuesday, the Fourth, when the professional pyrotechnicians will get out in the center of the lake, on a barge or some type of tugboat, and fire mortars, bottle rockets, and 8-inch shells into the humid sky, while Allison and Tommy and Crystal and Danny and all the kids will watch on the dock or the deck or in the yard. The kids will still be in their bathing suits, eating red, white, and blue cupcakes, and all the adults will be drinking screwdrivers out of red party cups, and it will feel like the night will never end, as the summers at Kerr Lake always are and always will be, and there will be Raed eating jail food, whatever that is, praying on his knees on the cold, cement floor, staring at a wall with no life. They'll leave their vacation lake home and return to regular home life. Tommy will go on selling overpriced homes in the Triangle, and at the Trinity Wellness Center, Allison will finally say goodbye to Mr. McFerlot, because he'll be ready to take on his rehab without the help of a physical therapist. What does "plotting a terrorist attack" really mean anyway? Raed from high school? Allison wouldn't have thought that in a million years. She'll wonder about it all and decide it was just a fling, but Raed will drift back to her mind every once in a while, because none of it feels right, how *those people* are treated and all, but the *N&O* will go back to writing about the $92 million Powerball jackpot and the controversial bathroom bill and pre-season ACC football and the Jihadists from Fuquay-Varina will become second- and third-page news and then forgotten for good.

Later that afternoon, Allison is in the kitchen starting the easy-bake lasagna and Tommy comes in from outside.

"You're red," she says.

"I fell asleep on the dock."

"Where are the kids?"

"They're fine. Playing and whatnot."

"Come here," she says, "Let me put some more sunscreen on you."

He sits at the large dining-room table, which is one of those artsy picnic tables designed for inside. The windows are ceiling high and have a view of the back deck and the yard that runs into the lake and the way the mighty pine forests turn and shift the shoreline, it looks like the lake goes on forever.

"You might blister," she says, taking her time to rub

the sunscreen on his back.

"I know it."

"You need a beer?"

"Probably need two."

He's a good man, she thinks. Tommy Taylor John. In a way, her life has become all of what she has imagined and hoped for: kids, the neighborhood and house, poolside summers and cookouts, the State Fair every October. Tommy's a teddy bear and wouldn't hurt a fly. She knows what he'll do even before he does, and isn't that something like love? Yes, Allison thinks, I love my life. It's all certain and safe. And shouldn't it be?

She wonders if maybe that was the whole point of Raed: to remind her to count her blessings. Thank God. Because there had to be a point to Raed the Jihadist. She kisses Tommy on the lips and gets three cold Coors Lights from the refrigerator. She cracks one open for herself. She looks out at the lake. What else in the world can I ask for, she thinks. She takes a sip. What can I do anyway? Call the police about it? Start a book club? The man's a terrorist. It still doesn't feel right.

Crystal and her family arrive just before dinner and they bring enough ice cream sandwiches for an army. They talk and laugh and catch up, and after the kids leave the table to catch lightning bugs in the yard, Tommy and Danny pour themselves whiskey and tell their wives they're headed outside to watch the kids.

"Did you get my message," Allison says after the men leave.

"What message?" Crystal moves to the refrigerator to make another vodka-cranberry.

"About Raed."

Crystal gives her a look. "Who?"

"Raed. From high school."

"Who?"

"You know: *Raa-eed*, the cute boy with the hazel-blue eyes."

"Allison, look, to be honest, I barely remember break-fast. The kids, work, one failed marriage, and one that's always hanging on by a thread."

"What happened?"

"Oh, nothing, you know what it's like. Men—"

"Are you and Danny all right?"

"Danny started to shave his pubic hair. He said he wanted to try something new. I said if I caught him cheating, I'd shave off something more than the hair on his balls."

"He's not, is he?"

"I don't think so. You know, it's probably just a phase. What is it, a mid-life crisis?"

"We're not ready for *that* yet, are we?"

"Lord," Crystal says, stirring her new drink. "I don't know. Maybe it's the crisis before the mid-life crisis. Or maybe he's been watching too much porn on the Internet. I don't know. How are you and Tommy?"

"We're fine," Allison says.

They clink their cups.

"Cheers," Crystal says.

"Cheers."

They both drink.

"So, now, who's this you keep talking about from high school?"

Allison hopes her text never goes through. If Crystal doesn't remember, maybe it really doesn't matter. Maybe it never really happened anyway. "It's nothing," she says, and reaches for more vodka. Her cup is half full, mostly cranberry juice. Could it be that simple, she thinks, to forget something or someone like that off the face of the Earth forever.

After she pours more vodka, they join the others outside, where the sun has finally faded beyond the lake's horizon. It will be night soon, but now islands of pink and magenta clouds cover the paling sky and the kids *ooh* and *aah* at the lightning bugs. It's all warm outside and there's a hint of breeze. Allison hopes there will be rain at least once over the next few days. She likes to hear water from the sky collapse on the lake.

Later, Allison will tell TJ to stop reading—for the third time—and play with Crystal's boys, who are eleven and eight and sporty and rough. Tommy will keep drinking whiskey and eventually he'll carry Eric to bed. Allison will tuck in Elizabeth. The kids will all be sleeping and the adults will have one more nightcap before bed.

Will there ever be an arraignment? Will it ever be clear what really happened at that house, what the "terrorist conspirators" acting as informants for Al-Qaeda really did? Will it matter? What about the women and children? But what does Allison have time for anyway? Lizzy wants to take horseback riding lessons and Eric needs to get into another sport because he's got too much energy and TJ, well, Allison wonders if he might be gay, which isn't necessarily a big deal anymore is it? Then there's Crystal's rocky marriage. Those are her priorities, what she is stubborn for.

It's all too much to think about. None of it in the world feels right, but does she have the time or energy to squeeze in anything else? She settles on: what a terrible story it all is.

When Allison and Tommy turn in for the night, they'll get under the covers and then Allison will ask Tommy to pull one of the curtains open just a bit because she wants to see the moonlight. Tommy will say he's sore and sunburned, but he'll get up to do it anyway, and then Allison will say, "Get the jelly from in the bathroom." She'll watch him move through the slightly moonlit bedroom and when he returns to bed, she'll listen to him squirt the lube and rub himself and say, "Are you ready," and Allison will lie on her back and say, "Let's do it quick before Lizzy comes in here," and when Allison feels her husband inside her, she'll breathe and relax and hope Crystal makes the cream cheese stuffed French toast she usually makes on this holiday weekend.

"A NIGHT AT OVELL'S CASINO"

The drifter arrived to Yanceyville on foot and brought with him some strange wind that forced the great oak on Main Street to uproot and collapse. Its roots were tangled like a bed of snakes. A few townspeople stopped to look and talk about how old the tree was and there was some pontification too, and then the sky turned charcoal and thunder shrunk the earth.

That afternoon Maurice Lipton staggered into Ovell's Casino at the edge of town and sat at the poker table. By eight o'clock his frown was heavier than thick, wet mud. "I'm losing bad," he said.

The dealer looked at him and said, "There's always the next hand, Mo."

"Don't start with all that."

The drifter entered the casino then. He had a clumsy disposition and moseyed about until he settled next to Maurice. "I've never seen weather like this before," he said.

Maurice gave him a hard look. "Who're you?"

The drifter extended his hand to greet Maurice.

"Good God!" Maurice said. "You got a few extra—"

"Fingers," the drifter said. "Yep . . . Five on one hand and seven on the other."

"Well, what in the—"

"Born with them. We're all born with a lot of wild and crazy things going on around us."

Maurice shook the drifter's hand. "Folks call me Mo. Who're you?"

"Nobody."

They played poker. Maurice drank whiskey and, after a while, the dealer asked if they'd heard about what happened to Joe Pickett.

The drifter shook his head no.

"Joe's the best man in town," Maurice said. "What happened?"

"Mo, his house is burning down," the dealer said.

"Say what now?"

"Yeah, something about the wiring inside the walls."

"Down on Price Street?"

"Mm-hmm. House caught fire after the rain started."

Maurice had had a wife and kids but he ruined that a long time ago. "Is Joe's family all right?"

"Don't know, but his house been burning all day in the rain."

"They can't put it out?"

"No, Mo. Been burning all day."

"My word."

"Did you say Price Street?" the drifter said then.

The dealer nodded yes.

"I just walked from there this morning before I came here."

"Huh," the dealer said, "is that right?"

Maurice looked at the drifter and then slowly twirled the bottom ring of his whiskey glass on the dark green poker table felt. He was drunk. "That's mighty strange," he said. "Say, where you'd say you were from."

"Nowhere really," the drifter said. "Burning in the rain. Ain't that the devil?"

Maurice looked at the walls then and wondered why everything in his life had fallen apart. "I need another whiskey."

"The way you're losing, that might not be a good idea," the drifter said.

Maurice looked at the walls again and thought they were shrinking. "It's too late to change now. Too late for sure." He felt sorry for it all.

"Well, you never know what the wind will bring," the drifter said and then he left.

"IF THAT ISN'T A SIGN FROM GOD, THEN I DON'T KNOW WHAT IS"

I'm from the red clay of the North Carolina Piedmont. From the loins of my Mama. It don't matter where I'm from, because it's for sure I can't go back, so I'm always thinking here we go.

Now I'm in Vegas, driving a limo I rented from a Chinese dude named Chu out in Henderson. And one night, this one guy down at the Venetian that I know calls me and says he has a guest I might want to pick up. It's almost midnight.

"What do you mean, 'might want to pick up,'" I say.

"Bill Joe," he says. His voice is raspy, and he puts you in the mind of one of them Italian mobsters from the movies. "Take it or leave it. We're all just trying to make a way out here, you know?" The world is full of interesting characters.

When I pull up to the lobby driveway, he nods to me and then gestures to a woman standing along the curb. I figure she isn't a day over thirty and everything she wears is tight and red. Her hair's thick and dark and little freckles dance on her olive skin. I get out all business-like and open the trunk. There's her red leather duffel bag on the hotel luggage cart. It's heavy, but not too bulky, not like what most women carry. I put it in the trunk and walk over to get the door for this woman, and as she steps toward the car, she reaches her arm and then her hand behind my neck, like to pull my head down like she wants to hug me, and sure enough, she does and then she plants a kiss on my cheek and says, "I've been waiting for you." It's more like a wet kiss and a whisper, and I think, here we go.

I nod to Little Miss Red and say, "Well, I'm here now." When I open the door, she slides into Chu's limo like she owns the thing and then she kicks off her high heels. The wind is whipping at me like it's God Himself telling me to mind.

Once I get into the driver's seat, I call her through the backseat speaker. "Ma'am," I say, "where to?"

She sighs and waits, and I start to repeat myself, but then she says, "Darryl, no games tonight. Let's go home."

Here's a question: what's heavier, divine intervention or sin?

I think I know the answer, so I push the Speak button on the control board, clear my throat, and say, "Ma'am, I think you have the wrong," but before I can finish she goes, "Darryl," and I'll never forget how she calls me like that, like I am the surest thing in the world.

I power the cabin window down and look at her in the rearview mirror. She's so cute and pretty, I think, watching her reapply her lipstick, and I haven't thought of a woman like that, in that way, in a long time, and she goes, "We made a lot tonight."

I haven't done nothing wrong yet. I don't say anything.

She goes, "I need a bath, a foot rub, and a brandy. Let's go home, Darryl."

Chu's limo has one of those fancy Sirius radios so I put it on the Jon Bon Jovi channel and turn that sucker up. I bet Little Miss Red is a 90s Rock type of gal, and anyway, who can't get into a song like "Living on a Prayer" going twenty miles an hour on the Vegas strip where all the neon makes the world feel like cotton candy. I don't right know where *home* is—or who this Darryl is—but that doesn't stop me from driving. I'm in it now, or I've decided I'm jumping in it.

I get almost to Circus Circus and Little Miss Red must have gotten antsy because she says, "Darryl, where are you going now?"

I say, "Sugar," not hesitating one bit, "the night's young. I thought you might've wanted to go one more round at the Riviera or the Sahara."

"Not tonight, love. I'm tired, and we won't make it to L.A. until morning."

"L.A.?" I say, although I don't want to say it like that. I retrace my tone. "I mean, you sure you want to go all the way to Los Angeles tonight?" I look at her then through the rearview mirror.

She gives me a look. "Home. Darryl," she says. "Home."

If you could talk to God and actually hear Him talk back like you could hear His voice and you knew it was His for sure, what would you ask Him? That's a question I think on when I'm juggling like I am with Little Miss Red.

I pull into a gas station and park. "You want a coffee or a Coke or something for the road," I say. She nods no and then I fiddle in the glove box and pull out the GPS. "Honey," I say, turning around to her through the cabin window, "you think you can plug in our address on this thing while I get some snacks. Remember how I got us next to lost last time."

At this point, I think I've messed the whole thing up, but what else am I going to do? What do you think, God? What else am I going to do? She stares at me hard, like she's testing me, but then she finally sighs like those she-she-foo-foo reality bitches on television do when what they mean to say is *I'm worth more than a hundred yous.* She leans toward me, takes the GPS, and says, "Darryl. Hurry, love."

If that isn't a sign from God, then I don't know what is. I hurry quick as all get-out, and inside the ARCO station I buy her two bottles of the Evian water (the expensive type), a few organic granola bars and a thing of

Greek yogurt that I think she might like, and a Red Bull, a pack of beef jerky, and a pack of Twizzlers for me. When I get back to the limo, I open the door, and she's sleeping. Out cold. I get the black fleece blanket from the trunk that this real old rich lady left in the cab recently and drape it over Little Miss Red. I almost kiss her on the forehead in that soft way I've kissed all the lovers I've had in my life, but don't. She did type the address into the GPS: 5690 Wilshire Drive, Beverly Hills, California.

When I reach the gate to the driveway, it's 4 a.m. and still dark as night. There's a code lock, and for a minute or two I mash buttons like I know the dang code. I get out, open Little Miss Red's door, and ease my hand back and forth on her forearm until she starts stirring.

"What is it," she says, waking up. I wonder if I'm still Darryl.

"It's the gate," I say, "I can't get the code to—"

"It's your birthday, Darryl," she says and sighs. "Remember?" She gives me a look then.

"Right." Well, I'm thinking, damn, now what?

I close her door gently and take out a cigarette. What I'm about to tell you makes no more sense than the man who hammers a nail up his nose. After I smoke half of my smoke, I go ahead and mash in my birthday 0-4-0-1 in the code box and the dang gate opens. Dag on, I think. I try not to act too surprised, thinking she might be looking at me through the limo window. I play it cool, like always, smoke the rest of my smoke, and get back in the driver's seat.

I've never been to Beverly Hills before, and, well, the houses are about as big and uppity as I expected. 5690 Wilshire has a circular driveway with a fountain statue of a little angel standing tippy-toe, spitting water from her mouth. When I pull around to the front of the house the motion light comes on and lights the home, which is more modest than uppity. It has two stories and is painted some fancy hipster color name for light-brown, something like Flirty Mocha or Burnt Tortilla.

Little Miss Red steps out of the limo barefoot like she's been in a long dream. "Darryl," she says, "don't forget the bag."

After I get her heels from the limo floor and her duffel bag from the trunk, I turn for the house, and she takes my free hand in hers. Our fingers intertwine like it's something familiar.

The front door's not locked. I let her lead me into the house and I drop the duffel bag at the foyer. She hands me her purse then and motions for her heels so I hand them to her. "Make us drinks," she says. "I'm going for a bath." She walks up the stairs then, one hand on the staircase banister, the other holding her red heels.

I'm just a Bill Joe. That's all what I'm thinking,

watching her move up the stairs smooth-like, like a fierce Catwoman. What would you do with a name like Bill Joe? She turns her head once at the top of the stairs to look down at me. She smiles. I stole 83 bases my junior year on the Varsity baseball team and that record still holds at our dinky high school ball field. William Joseph Ackley. Now, I'm just Bill Joe. I look up at Little Miss Red until she's out of sight and then I take her red purse and walk through the living room and on to the kitchen until I find the bar.

I pour myself a quick shot of Johnnie Walker. I don't particularly care for Johnnie Walker, but it's Blue Label Johnnie Walker so why wouldn't I? I open the purse and it has all the typical Little Miss Red paraphernalia, like lipsticks and a little mirror and mints and a make-up kit. There's nothing else worth looking at except her wallet. Little Miss Red is: Stacia Evie Worth. Eyes: Brown. Hair: Black. Height: 5'8". Age: 30. She's not a donor.

I'm exhausted and don't know my next move, but then I hear her yelling down to me from the upstairs so I rush to the foyer to hear her better.

"Stacia?" I say, taking a chance. "Honey?"

There's a pause and then she says, "I said, bring some chocolate."

"Oh," is all I come up with.

"Water's warm. I'm just waiting for you."

Next thing I know I'm upstairs rubbing Stacia's feet.

She's *ooh*-ing and *aah*-ing and saying how her heels were too tight. I'd be lying if I say I don't look at Little Miss Red's bare body between the soapy suds. You can dream a long dream about all the splashing and skin slapping that tub water is making on a girl like Stacia. All her innocent self there, fragile and naked in that tub. Why can't I just jump in there with her? Wouldn't you, God? Wouldn't you? I don't know yet just how sad it all is. We clink glasses and sip brandy, all the while I'm sitting on a stool there next to her by the tub. She looks so comfortable and I have a million-and-one questions that I can't yet just ask.

In between sipping and eating chocolates, she says, "Tell me a love story, Darryl, about us."

I decide to tell her a true story. I tell her about the time she almost sliced off her thumb cutting onions one evening in the kitchen.

She looks at her thumb then. "I did that?"

"Yeah, honey, don't you remember?"

She looks again at her thumb and then at me.

"Honey," I say, with a convincing tone, like I'm trying to convince her, make her as sure as she called me *Darryl* back in the limo in Vegas that this really happened. I'm awful. "It was my birthday. You were making your famous meatloaf. I was watching television downstairs and then you were yelling bloody murder from the kitchen."

"I did that?"

"Yeah, you did," I say. "I tried to take you to the

hospital, but you said you didn't want to ruin my big day. Remember?"

"I," she says, and I think she's bothered and confused, but really she's just putting that memory to life in that sick noggin of hers because she goes, "Oh yeah, I mean, I guess I did. I mean, you're sure, right?" Her skin is glistening wet and innocent in the tub water, and it's all beautiful and smells like pink and lilac and like your first time in bed with a woman. I'm awful and I think God has something to do with it. What makes a man make up something like that for a sweet girl like Stacia?

"Well," I say, "maybe you don't remember it like I do. I tried to take you to the hospital again and again and you finally told me to get the superglue from the garage."

She starts to smile then, like she remembers the whole dang thing.

"I went and got the superglue, and, well, you know the rest."

She looks at her finger again. "I didn't even cry, did I, Darryl?"

"Not one tear."

"Kiss me, Darryl," she says, and she's got that certainty in her voice again, like I'm her man.

I lean over the tub and soap bubbles wet my chin. She leans forward and we kiss and it's all mushy in her mouth and our tongues start to peck love pokes and jabs back and forth. After a while, Stacia pulls back and says,

"Darryl."

"Yeah, baby doll," I say.

"It'll always be like this, won't it?"

"Yeah, it is," I say, pouring a look over her. I'm like a bear sitting in a pool of honey.

She smiles. "Let's go lie down now."

She starts to stand then. The water's sprinkling and dripping everywhere. She's got the body of a goddess. I can't help myself but to look and then the strangest thing comes out of my mouth. It's like God is punching me in my throat. I say, "You want some eggs?"

She's not throwing her body at me, not that any woman ever has like that or ever will, that's just all fantasy isn't it, God, but she's looking at me and her look is doing a few different things: one is asking for something to dry off with, another is wondering why I'm asking about eggs, and then another is wondering why I'm still in my dress pants, shirt, and blazer after we've been home already and she's been all relaxed in the tub and whatnot.

I hand her the bathrobe that's hanging on the door. There are two there.

"Carry me to bed, Darryl."

I can hear my Mama telling me I'm no good as I try to swallow whatever God is trying to make me say.

"Come on, Stacia, you're not hungry?"

"Carry me, Darryl, like on our wedding night."

"I mean I can make a mean scrambled egg."

"Take me, Darryl. I'm ready for bed now."

I reckon I deserve a sick woman. All the hurt and worry I've put on everybody all my life.

"Let's lay together, Darryl. Please."

She's looking so pretty, and, dang, the way she says *please* like that. I take off my blazer finally and hang it where her robe was. The Man With No Past making scrambled eggs for The Insane-in-the-Membrane Crazy Lady. Together at last. "Giddy up," I say and I hold out my arms like to carry her. The water in the tub is talking as she starts to step up and then I lift her into my arms. All her wet innocence smeared on me like it's another type of baptism. I can tell her stories for ages. I'll just leave out all the heartbreak and she won't know no difference.

I carry her to the bedroom and notice the floors are hardwood, but everything else in the room is white. White walls, white bedside tables and white clothing drawers, even the California King is draped by a white-curtain canopy. I wonder if this'll be my deathbed one day.

"Darryl," she says, as I lay her down.

"Yes, baby doll."

"Meatloaf," she says. "Can we make meatloaf tomor-row?"

"Of course, Stacia," I say, and just like that, she's sleeping again. I tuck her in bed, make sure she's snug and warm enough. After that, I know what I have to do.

In high school I had a girlfriend who everybody thought was crazy. Her name was Darlene. I thought she was just unique. Someone interesting. More interesting than the rest of the world. She hated school worse than I did. She barely graduated. After lunch, she'd pick up the empty trays and trash students left on the cafeteria tables. Every day. I'd try to stop her, but she'd say, "You can tell a lot about people by the messes they make." Just strange stuff like that she'd say all the time. When I told Coach Taylor I was going to marry her as soon as we were both eighteen, he looked at me and said, "You know she's on the spectrum." I didn't know what that meant. He said, "She's as crazy as you are quick at running the bases." On a bet at a party the night of graduation I smoked 83 cigarettes because I was crazy about doing stupid shit. You can't help who you love or who you are, and that's the truest truth I know in the world. You can't help who you love or who you are. Let's just say it never worked out with me and Darlene but that's only because of how she died.

I go downstairs and finally open the duffel bag. It's full of cash, pills, and casino chips. Fifty thousand in cash or more, I figure. The pills are Vicodin, Sertraline, Risperidone, Donepezil, Memantine, and Zyprexa. I know the last one because my granny had dementia before she died, and that's the saddest death in the world to watch.

Daylight is probably another hour or so away. There

are too many unknowns. What if the neighbors come around? Or relatives? Shit, I'm not even for sure if this Darryl might not be on a jet plane or in a car coming back to 5690 Wilshire at any moment.

I take to the leather sofa in the living room because I need some shut-eye myself to think on things. I don't know why some memories stay with a person and some don't. Another lover I had had a broccoli-shaped birthmark on her inner thigh that I liked to nibble at and suck on, but I can't—for the life of me—recall what she really looked like. Wasn't she the redhead? What's weird is I remember everybody's phone number I dial. Why can't I trade that memory for the good stuff I've done in my life?

I fade away to sleep for a bit and dream of lightning bugs floating up to heaven. When I wake I have a stale taste in my mouth. The sun's beginning to shine through the big bay windows. It's quiet. That eerie quiet that's some sort of calm before the storm. I decide to call Mama.

After it rings for a while, she picks up.

"Mama," I say.

There's a pause that's like a wave getting ready to break.

"Bill Joe."

"Mama."

"You in trouble again?"

"No," I say quick. "How you doing, Mama?" I get up off the sofa and start to walk around the house.

"I'm fine. Just fine."

"Well, that's good, Mama." I make it to the foyer and then start down the long hallway that stretches to the back of the house.

"Where in the world are you anyway, Bill Joe?"

Framed photographs of a younger Stacia line the wall.

"Oh," I say, "I've been driving a limo in Vegas."

Mama exhales hard in the phone. There's Stacia in between her Mom and Dad at graduation. Stacia wears a navy blue gown, her smile charms the hell out of the camera.

"How's Tommy and June Bug?" I say.

"I've been worried about you," Mama says. "It's been a long time."

In another photo, a toddling Stacia sits on top of a yellow Labrador, like she's wanting to ride him. Her hair is lighter then and her skin is sun-kissed.

"I know, I know, I know. Don't worry on me, Mama. How's Tommy and June Bug?"

"They're fine, Bill Joe. Everybody's fine. Everybody." She exhales again, but it's a little softer. She wants a cigarette and so do I. I can hear Mama flipping through either a calendar or a notepad like she always does when she's sitting at the kitchen table on the phone. Like how I always remember her doing. In front of me is a picture of Stacia—probably nine or ten—holding a handful of blue ribbons at a swim meet. She's got buck teeth that look normal.

"*That's* not today, is it?" Mama finally says.

I know what she's talking about. In another photo, Stacia is in a sequined green dress, hugging onto a boy with the worst acne I've ever seen. He's in a tuxedo too with one of those cummerbunds.

"No, Mama, that's not today," I say.

She keeps flipping through whatever she's flipping through.

"Mama."

"What, Bill Joe?"

"Mama, can I come home?"

She stops flipping. I can hear her so good, it's like she's there in Beverly Hills at 5690 Wilshire Drive looking at me. Like I could reach out and touch her hand. I smile and think about driving back across the country in a limo I'm renting from a Chinese named Chu. Tommy and June Bug would laugh at how I'd tell it all. I could take a little bit of Little Miss Red's cash and send it on a money order to Henderson and just buy the dang thing. Dag on. I could set up something. A limo service to and from the State Fair. Or to a ball game or even to Kings Dominion and back. Everybody wants to ride in a limo at least once.

Mama says then, "I don't think that's a good idea, Bill Joe."

I should have taken a picture of me and Stacia last night by the tub. With her in my arms like we were married. Or, even better, like we were just in love with nothing else in the world. One of those selfie pics. After a few beats, I hang up on Mama.

I do take some of the cash. I could have taken all of it. I could have done a lot of things, if you think about it, and what do you think about that, God? When a man does what all might not have been expected, and considering what the woulda, shoulda, coulda is, it's way better. Is that still sin or divine intervention? I can't tell, because I don't hear God like that. I just feel him when he grabs my throat.

I'm The Man With No Past. Even my own Mama doesn't want me to come home. I write Stacia a note and leave it on top of her red duffel bag in the foyer. *You can't help who you are. Forget me not. Love, Darryl*

Here we go.

"SPREAD"

That white lady on TV got it all wrong, but it was funny as hell when her black Escalade got stolen. I was like, *WOW!* I mean, for real, she shouldn't have left her purse out on the porch like that.

On Monday night I'm watching a rerun of *The Haves and the Have Nots*—it's the one where Candace gets kidnapped and—Turtle and Malik are already sleeping—and that's when Leshanda calls and says, "Girl, Mr. Rucker's house is on HGTV," so I turn the channel. Folks like Mr. Rucker who own houses in Tha Hood about to get crazy money. Those boo koo bucks. I heard he already bought a house out in the valley twice as big as the one he had here in Long Beach. Why all of a sudden white people want to live on the Westside anyway?

I turn it on right when the blonde lady is holding the phone up to her husband's face since he's driving through our neighborhood. It's that show where they be buying people's homes and fixing them and then sell them. This bitch holds up the phone to him like she's afraid to touch him, which tells me everything. I bet he got to beg her for some ass. That's how she's holding it.

The husband's talking to this other white dude on the phone who says he has to talk to "his client" about their offer for 299,000 dollars. I'm like, damn, 299,000 dollars? That's some Hollywood bullshit though. Black folks in Tha Hood don't get agents like that, and besides everybody knows Mr. Rucker's already got a bunch of money hidden away somewhere, and even though he's still a Crip, he's not selling dope no more, so I don't know who the white lady's husband is really talking to.

They pull in the driveway and there's T-Boy's white minivan parked all crooked and up all the way against the metal gate. The wife says it looks like someone is home, but the husband tells her they can't just knock and check out the place because they got to get the owner's approval first. It's like there's some secret list he got that he ain't supposed to have. This bitch says the house looks too small and then the husband talks about the building in the back yard being real big and if it's legal—or "permitted" is what he says—then 299,000 dollars would be a steal. What he means is they about to get paid. He's all right cute for a white boy.

It goes to commercial and I call back Leshanda and ask her why Meisha keeps posting shit about people on Facebook instead of telling them to their faces. Meisha wrote "yall bitchz really need to spend time wit your kidsss itz ok #facts #badmotherscanthide #iseeu" and that's the third time she posted about how other people take care of they kids. Leshanda said Meisha has been on one lately since her mama-who-passed birthday coming up and she pops off when she gets in a mood. Like nobody else don't got shit they be dealing with. That's the problem with Social Media and Meisha. She don't think before she be posting. I know what's it like to lose someone so I just reply to her with an Amen emoji.

After the commercial, they fast-forward like a week and they're in our neighborhood again, this time walking to Mr. Rucker's porch. He's telling his wife they bought it for 320,000 dollars instead of 299,000 and they have to take it "as is." Mr. Rucker told them take it or leave it, and I already know what's inside the house before they even open the door. What really gets me upset though is how this white lady is looking inside like Mr. Rucker's life is a waste of time. She's saying *Eww gross* and *I can't believe somebody actually lived here.* When they get to one of the bathrooms, she goes, *Oh, my god,* and pauses like she really wants you to listen and then she goes, *This is so disgusting.* The cameraman zooms the camera in the bathroom, and it isn't that bad if you think about who all was living there, the tub and tiles just needs some scrubbing and the mirror needs cleaning, but there's a dookie turd floating in the toilet. I think what she's getting all worked up about is she can't imagine *herself* in that bathroom, but it's not like she's the one going to use it anyway, so why talk all that mess?

I know she isn't going to like the bedrooms neither. Mr. Rucker made all the bedrooms in the house the same. There's three of them. All the same size and have the same dark green carpet and deep blue walls. They each got a bed frame and mattress, a window, a mirror, a closet, and a dresser drawer. What all you need to make a room yours. Now the kitchen—which everybody shared like the bathroom—is a mess, I'll give the bitch that much. Beer cans and empty bottles of liquor and glasses on the counter, dishes in the sink, takeout Chinese and Jack In The Box wrappers that've been there a while. There are a few dirty pots and somebody left something in a grease-stained skillet on the stove and then a rat runs through the room and that bitch starts screaming like she's getting stabbed. She runs tippy-toed out the house in her heels and the husband is just shrugging and sighing like the rat isn't that big a deal and you can tell he knows he messed up marrying such a prissy-ass bitch.

I know Mr. Rucker has them same orange plates and cups in the kitchen cabinets since when I used to go by there to help him clean up the place. I started going around to Mr. Rucker's when my Uncle Mosey got out of prison. I was seventeen and in the eleventh grade. Uncle Mosey didn't have no money, but he and Mr. Rucker used to run together, and that's when Mr. Rucker started making some real money and he made his house a place men could go when they got out of prison or the halfway house, like my Uncle Mosey. When me and Mama went up the street to visit Uncle Mosey, Mama would always take him a fifth of erk and jerk, a can of ginger ale and some gummy bears, and Uncle Mosey would make us Prison Spread in Mr. Rucker's kitchen.

Uncle Mosey would always be hassling me, like, "Come on, Charlie," he'd say, "it'd be nice if you could come up in here and clean up for your Uncle. Help your Uncle out." Only Uncle Mosey called me Charlie—not Charlene—because he always teased me about how he swore I looked like a boy because of my bowlegs and I didn't like to wear no girly clothes neither. I loved my Uncle Mosey—my Mama's brother—so I said yes.

It was easy. I went every Tuesday after school. Mr. Rucker made sure everybody was out of the house so I could clean without being disturbed. He gave me all I needed to do the job. He paid me fifty dollars and then when I got pregnant the first time, he let me go three days a week since I quit going to school then. After I lost that baby, I knew I wasn't going back to school. At night, I worked at Tootsie's on Willow and still cleaned for Mr. Rucker every Tuesday, and then I met Travis and we started hanging out back behind Mr. Rucker's house in his work shed. That's where everybody in the neighborhood went late night. Mr. Rucker used to work on trucks—or whatever it was—but he kept so much machinery and metal scraps in the backyard you'd think he was one of them hoarders. He said it was all worth a lot, which is why he kept Bones his pit bull tied up there in the back outside the work shed, and Mr. Rucker said he was selling it all piece by piece at a time, but that's where we'd kick back, smoke a little smoke, get our dance on, just chill, kick back.

"This is either going to be really good or really bad," the husband says to his wife when they go through the back door and see all the scrap metal and are standing at the door of Mr. Rucker's work shed. It's taller and wider than the house, that's for sure. The husband can barely get the door open wide enough, it's jammed or stuck, so he tells his wife she should squeeze through and see what's blocking it, and she says, "You think I'm going to go in there first?"

My Mama was a ho too, but I don't say that like it's a bad thing. These niggas out here brag about getting ass like they got gold dick, so why can't bitches sling too? My Daddy was married to a white woman, but he always gave my Mama what she needed. He was with us enough of the time. After he died, Mama told me, "Your Daddy was a rolling stone." She was never the jealous type and didn't try to beat on Daddy or hurt him because he had other women. Mama loved Daddy. So did I.

Travis was the same. It was just me and him at first. I was nineteen, still working at Tootsie's and he told me one night I could make a lot more than a few hundred a week on tips at the bar. When he said, "You got to just trust me, Charlene," I knew I would. I wanted him like that. To tell me what to do. Protect me. I loved how he called my name. We were at Mr. Rucker's the first time. He took me through the work shed to one of the back rooms. There was still a mess of metal all around, but there was nice lighting and Travis set me on the bed and kissed me and told me he'd be right there and wouldn't let nobody hurt me. It was easy. Travis waited outside the room—or outside the work shed. I never kissed anybody on the lips except for Travis and mostly no one wanted to kiss anyway. *Put that ass out* or *I want to hit it from behind*, that's all a nigga wants to say to you when they pay you for it. It was always quick, and I never sucked dick unless they paid double—that's what I told Travis I'd do it for, double. Travis didn't like me to do that though anyway. He said that's a sure way to get herpes or something worse. Travis never fucked me hard like that. He'd make love to me and kiss me on my mouth and tongue kiss me and take his time with me. He was never hard on me like some of these other niggas who got wives at home and still pay bitches to fuck and then go to church on Sunday.

The husband finally pushes his way through the door and opens the garage to the work shed, which is rusty and the motor shakes when it moves. They look around at all the scraps and empty paint tins and old truck batteries and the husband curses and even though the show edits it out, you can tell he said, "Mother fucker." I bet he was thinking all the racist shit white people think about when they get near Tha Hood and wonder about black people. Wonder what it's like to live off of food stamps and government cheese. Wonder how in the world we could have ever created people like Prince and Beyoncé and Whitney Houston. Nobody was like Whitney. Celine Dion is the only white lady who sings like she got some black in her.

That reminds me about this white girl from high school who said in class one day that the reason why Rodney King got beat was because he *actually* was a felon who *actually* robbed and beat up a Korean man. She said that was some kind of karma. Everybody wanted to kick her ass, but she dated Shawn Motts—who was the best athlete at our school and got a scholarship to some fancy school to play basketball. She thought because she was dating a black guy she could just say what all the fuck she wanted and it would be all right. She was talking about Rodney King getting beat by police like it was something in ancient history, like how white people say black people can't still be mad about slavery because it was so long ago. That was the other reason I didn't go back to school after Travis had me turning tricks for him.

I couldn't believe those rooms were still there in the back of Mr. Rucker's work shed. Travis had other girls and I knew that too, but once I got pregnant with Turtle, Travis started saying he didn't think the baby was his, and I told him it had to be because he was the only man I let cum up in me. He paid for the test though and that proved it. I told him I wanted to stop, and he said he needed me to make a little more money, so I still turned until I was four months and started showing. I think it hit Travis then, that he was about to be a father. I could tell Travis loved me because he told me he did and he made sure I always had what I needed and he went with me to the doctors, and he wanted me to stay up at the house with Mama, like it was, like, some kind of womb, and it was only a matter of time before our son came into the world. Travis brought a baby crib and already starting getting him Jordans. He said he wanted Turtle to be a junior. I couldn't say no.

Travis went away before Turtle was born. Only Travis calls him Junior. Everyone else calls him Turtle because of how long it took him to be born. Thirty-two hours in labor. His heart ain't right either, so he's something like slow, and if I'm honest it's probably because I didn't stop drinking when I was pregnant. I needed a drink after Travis went away. My pastor says I got to talk about it, be honest about it, but I'm not sure that even matters. All that matters is my son's heart keep beating.

When they're inside the bedrooms at the back of Mr. Rucker's work shed I can't believe they still haven't put it all together about what Mr. Rucker's house really was: a halfway house in the front and a party place in the back. It's not that difficult to see. The husband says some stupid shit too, like, he says out loud, "I wonder if we're going to find somebody dead back here."

Black people got manners. That's how we're raised. Even Malik, who's three, knows how to greet people when he enters a room. We take the time to raise a child. Teach him how to be respectful and polite. Malik's daddy isn't Travis and Turtle knows that too, and, you know what, they still brothers.

Somebody did die though at Mr. Rucker's. It was on the street outside his house. I went back to turning tricks after Turtle turned two. Mama was looking after him at the house. She knew I went back to work, but she didn't say anything about it. One night I was in the back at Mr. Rucker's with a little young nigga whose homeboys gave me two hundred dollars and told me to do him until he couldn't stand straight. I was twenty-three. This little nigga wanted to kiss me on the mouth and my neck and he tried to go down on me, so I put it on his face. Gave it to him. After a while, I could tell he couldn't take it anymore, he wanted it so bad, so I let him stick it in me. I could feel his little boney hips when he pushed in on me, and then we heard gunshots that sounded like they were coming right through the work shed. We dropped to the floor and just lay still there until it was quiet. Then he rushed to put on his clothes and he went out first. After I got outside, I could hear sirens on Santa Fe and one of his homeboys was lying there on the asphalt already dead.

Uncle Mosey had to go back to prison too. He and Travis are in the same penitentiary. Spread is easy to make. All you need is two or three packs of ramen noodles, a small bag of Chili Cheese Flavored Fritos, hot sauce, a few mustard packets, a can of chili beans, and some kind of Easy Cheese. Uncle Mosey says it's easy to get inside when he's got money on his books, but Travis says he wouldn't eat it even if he had all the money he could have on his books. He says he's watching what he's eating and exercising every day, a few times a day. I believe him. Mama helps me put a little money on his books every other month or so. He might get out by the time Turtle will be a grown man, but I'm not one of those fake hos who thinks her man is getting out sooner than he is. The law would just as soon see a nigga stay in the pen and break him down so when he gets out all he does is think about how to get back. Speaking of fake hos, I wonder how this white lady makes macaroni and cheese. I bet the noodles are too dry and the cheese is hard. What's probably more true is I bet this bitch probably doesn't even cook at home. Makes her husband do it.

They're making their way back to the front of the

house when the husband says, "Wait, is that our truck I hear?" She goes for her purse, but she doesn't know where it is. He's like, "Why don't you know where your purse is?" She's frantic and panicking, like she's about to drown in the back of Mr. Rucker's with all that scrap metal, and they run out to the driveway, and, yep, somebody stole their truck and is driving down the street. What's even funnier is that there are people on the street watching, like they saw the whole thing happen, and you can bet if the police start asking questions, they ain't gonna say shit.

The white boy runs after the truck, which is even more funny, and whoever is driving is fucking with him, going slow so he can catch up and then he speeds up the street. It goes to commercial like that, with the white boy running after his Escalade and the wife yelling, "Be careful, honey."

When I was little, Daddy and Uncle Mosey took me fishing at the pier downtown. That's where the world meets. Everybody got the same goal down there, to catch something. After Daddy died and before Uncle Mosey went to prison, Uncle Mosey said he didn't know too many girls who liked fishing like I did.

"Why not?" I said.

"It's just not something girls are known to do."

Uncle Mosey told me about his granddaddy—my great granddaddy—and how they were the first Negro family to own a home in Holmes County, Mississippi. That's how Uncle Mosey called our people—Negro. He said he was going to move back there, find the house, buy it again, fix it up, make it a nice bed and breakfast, maybe make a garden, corn and tomatoes and some other vegetables. Uncle Mosey always caught more fish than anybody else out there at the pier. The Chinese, the Samoans, the Mexicans, everybody. White people were the worst. Uncle Mosey said it was the bait that did it.

"They too stingy, but it's easy, really," he said, "You got to just hook the bait so it looks better to the fishes down there than everybody else's."

When the show comes back on, they've gotten their car back. Leshanda says what happened was insurance paid for them to get a brand new one. She says they found that truck out somewhere near Bakersfield, stripped and gasolined.

So, they've cleaned out all that shit at Mr. Rucker's house. All that scrap metal and wiring and whatever else was in the back. I don't know what happened to Bones, but I stopped going to Mr. Rucker's all together after I saw that dead boy on the street. I stopped working like I was doing. I went back to Tootsie's and started braiding hair during the day for one of my Mama's girlfriends who owns a salon on Atlantic. That's how come I met Malik's Daddy—Hassan. He's the brother of another girl who braid hair at the shop. He's been in jail, but he ain't going back. We don't feel the same about each other, but he's a good daddy. He takes Turtle with him when he takes out

Malik over the weekend or even during the summer when he gets Malik for a few weeks. Malik won't go anywhere without his brother. It started when Malik came back crying and saying he'll only go if his brother can go, and what can you say to that?

Five and three. Two boys. Me raising boys to be men. Strong, black men, not no niggas like out here in Tha Hood. They dolled up that house and sold it for almost five hundred thousand dollars. And the thing is, they sold it to a white family, and there goes the neighborhood. I told Hassan to take Malik and Turtle fishing this summer at the pier downtown.

"Fishing?" he said, "why fishing?"

I told him that's the only place in the world where everything is equal. I told him if he doesn't take them fishing, then I would, and I don't care how stupid we'll look taking the bus either with all our fishing gear. My boys will learn how to fish. I'll bet all Mr. Rucker's money on that.

"WHAT'S HEAVY"

Downstairs in the TV room, the WRAL weatherman Bob Debartly, whose head is about as big as a watermelon, is talking about Hurricane Federico. Dad is sprawled on his lazy-boy recliner. Two IVs are plugged into his left arm, both are murder red, and I can't ever tell which is sucking blood and which is pushing in. The dialysis machine is beeping and thudding like it always does.

"How much y'all win by last night?" Dad says.

"9-1."

"How many hits you get?"

I should tell Dad about the perfect bunt I laid down the third base line in the second inning so Mike Poole could get to third and Brandon could get to second, but Dad always used to say *Swing like you mean it.* "Walked three times," I say. "Scored twice."

"Dang, Dickie. You couldn't get a hit against that rag-muffin squad?"

I should tell him I'm quitting baseball. "It's not my

fault they can't pitch," I say instead. "Walking is the only sure way to get on base."

Dad looks at me, eyes bloodshot. "Well, reckon you're right. It's just not as pretty is all." The machine goes crazy for a minute, beeping and breathing and vibrating, and Dad adjusts one of the knobs. He's the only reason I still play ball.

Mom's car isn't in the driveway. I grab a pack of Pop-Tarts and a glass of orange juice and go back upstairs to play *Call of Duty 2*. I shoot the shit out of Nazi Germany for a while and then Dad calls for me and I go back down. His breath is sweet and sharp and wet and a bottle of Jim Beam is shoved at the back of his recliner.

"Son," he says, "can you change this out?"

His waste bag is full and gross looking. I unplug the plastic tubes, and the bag of human waste feels ready to explode. Dad mumbles he's going to bed soon. It's not even noon.

I walk upstairs to the blue bathroom. After you do it a few times, it's like anything else in the world. I set the plastic bag of piss and whatnot in the sink and pull on the rubber gloves from the cabinet that's stocked full of any and everything medical. Mom even puts condoms in there: a box of LifeStyles "ribbed for her pleasure." I don't know if she left them there for me or what, but that's not a conversation I'm going to have with her. Once I put the gloves on, I pull the cork from the bag and pour it all down the toilet. I've only had a spill or two.

Stacia texts me then. *Hey.*

I text her back. *Hey.*

There's a pause and I know she's writing something either good or bad, and then I get the message: *I think you're so sweet, Dickie, it's just . . .*

I don't have to read the rest.

I text Doug: *Mall?*

A few minutes later, Doug texts back: *Inception at 1:30? I'll be in the driveway.*

It's funny how people only care about stuff when they have to. The Outer Banks always gets hit with hurricanes, but folks out there know how to deal with it. The least they do is board up their windows. In the driveway, I look up and there's not a cloud in the sky. Our neighbor is mowing his grass.

When Doug pulls in the driveway, I get in his car and the weather guy on the radio says, "Hurricane Federico will be just a little summer shower by the time it hits Wake County." Doug changes the channel then and later, when we're almost at the mall, he says, "You're coming to the party tonight, right?"

I nod yes and then say, "You're not worried about the storm?"

He shakes his head. "Hell no," he says.

We eat pizza at Sbarro and then walk through the mall. The hallways are wide, the floors fake marble, and the warm yellow of all the fluorescent lights makes me yawn. We pass Victoria's Secret and the model on the poster ad is staring at me: green eyes, dirty blond hair pouring over her tits like a waterfall. She's on the floor, bored, lying there in her red thong. I see Ophelia from math class—we've been in the same math class since fifth grade. She's sifting through a pile of panties at a sale counter. Everything is pink in there. Ophelia's wearing baggy sweatpants and our Athens High hoodie, but really she's got firm thighs and a nice, gushy booty. I know because she's caught me staring at her in gym class before. I start to get a semi, and then Doug says: "You bring any booze?"

"Huh?"

"You bring any booze for the movie?"

I shake my head no. "Tonight, man," I say.

He gives me a look.

We've each seen *Inception* at least three times. We don't talk about the ending, but Doug knows already how I feel about it. The last time we saw it, we were stoned off some skunky weed Doug bought from a Mexican kid at school. I told Doug I thought Cobb was dreaming it all: his kids there in the back yard on the clean, green grass. "That's why the top was still spinning," I said.

"Dickie, what the fuck are you talking about?"

"If he wins, what's the point of the movie?"

"Jesus Christ, Dickie. Stop being an asshole. You're just high. DiCaprio wins. He beats the bad guys. Sometimes, it's just that simple."

After the movie, we walk through the mall again before we leave. I feel like an idiot when we pass Victoria's Secret and I stare in there looking for Ophelia. It's been at least two hours. We make our way out and Doug drops me back at home. "See you tonight," he says.

There's still no sign of a storm, and Mom's car isn't in the driveway. Inside, the house smells like a sewer and Dad's machine is screaming. I hear him in the kitchen. "Dad," I say, "what—"

"Nothing, Dickie," he says, "Damn it. Ain't nothing wrong. Go on to bed."

"It's five-thirty," I say. I walk into the kitchen and see how frail Dad is. His shirt and pants are soaking wet. "Dad, why didn't you wait for me—"

"I ain't waiting for nobody, son. Nobody and nothing."

I move to him and he sort of pushes me, but I ignore it and throw his right arm around my neck. On the kitchen counter there's vomit and in the sink the tubes and the plastic waste bag. The tubes were stripped out. Dad's mumbling fuck this and fuck that. I walk him to his lazy-boy recliner, but it's just as soiled as his pants so I walk him to the guest bedroom downstairs where he's been sleeping. I lie him down on the bed and take off his pants and shirt. He's choking now and I hate his breathing on me. His briefs sag on his hips. I slide them off and he's all shriveled down there. I try not to look, but his one nut is just sitting there, like it's waiting for some other body.

His clothes are on the floor and Dad's naked and snoring on the bed. I get a cloth from the bathroom and wet it and wipe him down and dress him in a pair of nurse's scrub pants the hospice people gave us. I find a long-sleeved flannel and button him up and try to tuck the covers around him.

Mom comes home just as I finish cleaning up the kitchen. She's still in her zumba clothes. "Richard," she says, "are you burning incense?"

"Dad had an accident," I say. "I'm going to Doug's tonight."

She walks to the living room and I meet her there. We're facing each other. The swoosh of the ceiling fan above us. She gestures to the recliner. "Why didn't you clean this up?" she says.

I swear the damn recliner is drooling feces. "That?" I say.

Her body slants and the distance between us swells. I picture her at zumba, moving and bouncing in her tights that are too tight and skimpy for a soon-to-be widow and I get even more mad. "Mom," I say, "what the—"

"Richard," she says.

"Mom," I say louder.

She starts waving her arms and breathing heavy like she's drowning or something and she starts saying all the stupid, shitty things she says when she gets shitty with me.

I hate her now.

"I cleaned *him* up," I say, "and the kitchen too. That recliner smells like shit. It smells like—"

"Goddammit, Richard!" she says.

I quit it then.

So does Mom.

We're quiet and barely facing each other.

The fan drones, but the stink doesn't move.

I want to tell Mom it's about the worst thing in the world to always feel lonely, but then we both hear what sounds like Dad falling. She runs to the room and leaves me with the recliner.

Outside, it starts to rain.

"I'm taking the car, Mom," I say. "I'm staying over at Doug's tonight." I don't care if she hears me. I grab the extra set of keys from the wooden key hook that reads *HOME*.

The wind is blowing hard now, the raindrops like lead.

Debartly and the others got it all wrong. It's not even midnight but I can't tell for sure because the light on my watch doesn't work. I'm in the kitchen pantry of Doug's house with Ophelia, and she's wearing some sort of see-through skintight pantyhose. I move my hands up and down her thighs.

"Don't go so fast, Dickie," she says. Her voice is sweet

like cheesecake.

I slow down. Try to relax and all, but it's tough because I don't know how much time I have. The storm outside sounds like it's on the other side of the pantry door even though Doug lives in Lochmere where all the houses are made of marble and granite and sturdy hardwood and the grass is always trimmed and there's not a stray leaf or limb anywhere in the yard.

"That's it," Ophelia says, and her breath on my neck makes everything get heavy and hot, and then she goes, "Yeah, just like that," like she wants me to taste each syllable.

How we got here in the pantry is Hurricane Federico broke the big bay windows in Doug's living room. Before that, it was like every other party at Doug's house: cases of beer and liquor bottles on the kitchen counter, drinking games going on—something like Thumper or Quarters, music blasting out everything. Then the storm rushed in and broke the windows and everyone cursed and ran through the house to find a safe place. Someone yelled, "Get to a durn bathtub. That's where it's safe, y'all." I grabbed Ophelia's hand and we dove into the pantry.

"What do we do now?" I said.

She giggled. The wind rattled the door. We could hear glass shattering, and then I started to sort of touch her and she didn't stop me.

We're safe, the only thing is I have to piss. I almost say

something to Ophelia, but she says, "Dickie Shoemaker, tell me a secret."

It's so dark in here, even Dad wouldn't be able to tell that Ophelia is black.

"Come on, Dickie," Ophelia says, "tell me something no one knows. Pretend it's our last night alive."

I've never been with a black girl, but I know I can't say that, and I can't think of any deep, dark secret worth telling, so I say, "Your brother would kick my ass if he knew we were in here."

She sucks her teeth and sort of stiffens for a second, but my hands are still moving on her thighs. "Mike's not like that," she says.

"Like what?"

"He doesn't look over me like he's got to beat up any boy who talks to me. He's just my brother."

"Unh-unh," I say. "You can't get with your teammate's sister in the closet."

I feel her start to feel me. We're leaning in between shelves of canned goods and extra *things* that Doug's mom must have bought in bulk at Sam's Club.

"What do you mean *get with*," she says like she's messing with me, and she's really feeling me. All this while the wind is whirling and the rain is hammering the roof, and I have to piss. "We haven't even kissed," she keeps on, "We're just in the pantry waiting out the storm, right?"

I don't say anything, just keep moving my hands slow

like she told me to, and then she says, "Who'd you *get with* last, anyway?"

"Stacia," I tell Ophelia. It's a lie I'll get away with.

"You got with Stacia Spelling?"

I pause and then I move my head in close to her neck and nibble on her earlobes. "Yeah," I say. "I mean not like *that.*"

"You just fooled around with her?"

I say *mm-hmm* and there's a weird mixture of smells—Ophelia's citrusy perfume, rolls of toilet paper, and packs of Nabs, all while the wind's still howling.

Our heads are nuzzled up real close to each other and Ophelia starts to play with my hair. I'm kissing all over her neck.

"She's all right, I guess," Ophelia says.

I don't say anything.

Ophelia's still rubbing me and she likes how I'm nibbling on her and then she keeps on about Stacia. "I mean, she's nice and all, I guess, I just never thought you—"

I stop Ophelia because I don't really care and I push my lips on hers, and then she draws back like she's looking at me, but our faces are still close enough to kiss.

"What is it?" I say.

"Nothing," she says real soft, like she's whispering, and I can taste her breath, and then she brings her lips back to mine and we make out while we're still feeling on each other. Our teeth clink, but it still feels good.

Ophelia's lips are juicier than any orange I've ever eaten. She sucks on my bottom lip like it's a lollipop, and I've never had a girl kiss me and do like that, but I hope every girl I ever get with from now on does like this. I try to suck on hers the same way and then the thunder rumbles so hard I can feel it in my chest.

She draws back. "You know I saw you looking at me at the mall today."

"When?" I say like I don't know what she's talking about.

"Today. You were there with Doug."

I hold her a little tighter and say, "I was there."

"You were watching me?"

I sort of laugh and go back to kissing her. I try to suck on her bottom lip again and then I drive my tongue all through her mouth like it's telling her how bad I want her. Our tongues bang and slap at each other back and forth.

"Dickie Shoemaker from math class, you're a freak, huh?" she says. "Watching little ol' me buying panties—"

I kiss her hard again. "Which ones did you get?"

We both laugh and I try to forget about peeing, but it's starting to sting.

"You think you're going to find out tonight?" she says and she's teasing me.

"I hope so." I slide my fingers higher up her thigh and

play with the seams of everything. I reach through to her skin and it's soft and smooth. I'm moving, going closer and closer. I kiss her harder and harder, and I can't hear the storm anymore because I have to piss so bad, but all I can think about is tearing off the panties Ophelia bought at Victoria's Secret.

She starts to play with my belt buckle, like she wants to unbuckle it and then she stops. "Dickie," she says, "is that your leg shaking like that?"

"Huh?"

"Are you—" she says, and then we fall.

I couldn't hold my stance any longer.

Ophelia laughs. There's more thunder. We're sprawled on the pantry floor and it's pitch black. My legs feel like there's a million needles sticking in them. They fell asleep. My legs. They just gave out. Ophelia was ready and all and then I fell and I can't explain how I always fuck shit up.

"Ophelia," I say.

"Yeah?"

"I have to pee."

I feel her giving me a look.

"There's a hurricane going on outside, remember?" she says. "Everyone else is in the bathroom anyway."

It's stinging so bad I can't hold it anymore.

"Wait," she says then, "I have an idea."

"Huh."

"Let's find a bottle."

We stand and rummage the shelves. She finds an empty two-liter plastic bottle. "Here," she says.

I take it and turn, then unbuckle and unzip my pants. My hard-on went soft already. It's still raining and thundering. I try to get the head of my johnson as close as I can to the tip of the bottle without directly touching it. The bottom of the bottle gets warm and then my piss *pees* and *pish*-es everywhere.

"Gross," Ophelia says, "you're so loud."

All I think to say is, "What'd you expect," like I'm trying to be funny.

When I finally finish I twist on the cap and put the bottle on the shelf behind me.

I move to face Ophelia and I wish she was straddling my leg and I was nibbling on her earlobes like before and Ophelia moves to face me too and grabs hold of my waist like she's going to hug me, but it's sexier than a hug.

"Ophelia," I say. "I got it."

"What?"

"The secret."

I feel her all over me. "Yeah," she says. There's a giddiness in her voice.

"I wish my dad would go ahead and die."

She breathes, and I notice her exhale is real heavy, just as heavy as the truth I just told her, just as heavy as my piss in the two-liter plastic bottle on the shelf behind me, just as heavy as the wind and rain outside. She reaches up on her tippy toes and kisses me on the lips, but it's not a kiss like you put on someone you're getting with in the pantry closet during a hurricane.

"Dickie," she says, and it still feels like she's exhaling, like she's doing that for me.

I don't say anything. I just keep hold of her, and then I say, "I hope Federico tears it all down."

"Don't hope that," she says. "Come here. Kiss me, Dickie. Come on."

We kiss then, and I can tell she's trying to get us where we were before I had to stop to piss. The wind's getting louder again, I can feel it.

"THE GARBOLOGIST"

You think you know how this will end. It's some morning after it all happened. It doesn't matter how long ago it actually happened, but what does matter is that this is the morning when you're ready to move on. Turn over a new leaf, as they say. Before now, you hated that saying and whoever would ever say that in the first place, but sometimes a cliché becomes something real again.

You're at the "TRASH," but it's not actually trash or a trash can or any variation thereof, it's a cardboard box that's sort of closed, but sort of always opened, and on each side it reads "TRASH," because it's full of the shit that you kept, remnants of him, and you don't know why you kept it, but at the time it seemed like the only rational thing to do and at the time it seemed to prove something. (That word "seemed" is always a mirage.)

Shit like:

- Ticket Stubs (*The Phantom of the Opera*: you hate the opera, but you thought he thought you were artsy or something like that, so you told him you wanted to go, but really you just wanted to fall asleep with him somewhere in public to see how he might hold your hand and if he snored or not (your palms smeared together so hard it was like you were making love, and no, he didn't snore); movies: mostly action or drama flicks at Carmike Cinemas, and there's a stack of them, and you two had your routine of smoking a joint before any and every movie and you snuck in a plastic bag full of stovetop popcorn and four Natty Lights—two for each of you; sporting events: whatever, you'd rather watch porn or reruns of *The Golden Girls*)

    - Homemade and Hallmark Cards (*Happy Anniversarys*, *Thank Yous*, *I'm Sorrys*, *Congratulations*, funny cards with animals doing animal things that translate somehow into something human (human means what again?))

    - Sacred Things (the ______________ that he __________ with; pictures of you and him at the beach, in the mountains, somewhere in Europe, in a photo-booth; the ____________; more pictures (this time framed) of you (you look cute) and him (he looks, well . . .); that ____________; the pack of cigarettes you two stole from the 7-Eleven the night you were really, really drunk, and while neither of you smoke, it was a dare and it was fun; the beads: beaded necklaces, bracelets, more necklaces, ahem . . . anal beads that were a joke at first, but ________________ (why do beads somehow equate to love?)

There's more shit. Piles of it. You sift through and wonder how you two ever lasted that long, but then you find something at the bottom of the box that's now really just a box because it's almost empty and the trash part of it is lying on the floor all around you.

The something is a manila folder. You open it (again). Inside there are two pieces of paper. You try to read both, but you don't get past CERTIFICATE on either. You decide to put all the shit back in the box and cross out the words "TRASH" with a black, permanent marker like you've done a few times before. (You think: what doesn't kill you will make you stronger.)

"INFORMAL LETTER WRITTEN BY A STUDENT TO HER ENGLISH TEACHER WHILST HAVING TOO MUCH TIME LEFT OVER IN GYM 2 AFTER FINISHING THE SAT WAY TOO EARLY"

Dear Mr. Sturdivant,

This is Amanda from English 12. I know letters don't usually have titles like the one above, but you always say we should give a clear title to everything we write, so there you go. I'm only typing this now because when I finished hand-writing a draft of this right at 12:50 on scrap paper, our exam proctor, this old lady who wore everything wool and smelled like fart dust, said we couldn't take any papers out of the room—even our scrap paper—and I really wanted to finish this because I have to finish what I start, no matter what.

In case you're wondering, fart dust is a term Jeremy Russell made up. At least he said he made it up. Fart dust is like perfume. As Jeremy Russell puts it, "It mists from your anus and sticks to your clothes so it follows you wherever you go," and that's a direct quote. It's not too awful-smelling like a stink bomb, I mean fart dust isn't, it more just sort of lingers like a malodorous shadow (*malodorous* is a high-level SAT word). Sometimes I get a whiff of fart dust when I hug my Grandma and that makes me afraid to get old. Jeremy Russell is about the grossest boy I've ever met, but at least he's nice most of the time and honest. You know he won't hurt you.

How do you feel about the word *whilst*? I feel like it's a word that people probably either love, hate, or are confused about. I get it though. *Whilst* is just the British way of saying *while*, which is to say it's the fancy-pants way of saying *while*. The opposite of something fancy-pants to say would be *I reckon*. I wonder what British people would say to that transitive verb, Mr. Sturdivant. I can think of about a million things people around here say that would confuse the mess out of British people in the same way *whilst* confuses the whole of Wake County. Maybe that's why we won the American Revolution or maybe that's why the British lost. Either way, *whilst* was sitting there on one of the reading comprehension questions of the SAT. There was a passage from something one of the Brontë sisters wrote.

Do you believe in ghosts, Mr. Sturdivant? On the topic of paranormal activity, I believe the same as I do with extraterrestrials. Does anybody really know if either exists? Does it matter? Maybe it only matters what you believe in.

Wait, now, I don't want to be caught in a lie. I take

some of that back. *Whilst* I do think ghosts exist, *I reckon* I don't really care about extraterrestrials. And space for that matter. And especially movies about space, space travel, the future, or hobbits (who aren't real). Why do boys care so much about all that mess? Like, the entire boy population. The nerdy-math-Asian boys who all wear glasses. The geeky-environmental-science boys who have pet frogs and wear tethered Birkenstocks. The redneck boys who hang out in their big Dodge trucks at the Sheetz on Avent Ferry Road. Even the untouchables, like Tucker Brigley and Billy Pitt (more about them later). I will say I did like the movie *Interstellar*, but only because I love Matthew McConaughey. He's the type of guy I want to marry one day. But, please, don't take me on a date to see any *Star Wars* episode. Ever. I do believe in ghosts though, because Aunt Mildred visits me every once in a while in my bedroom when I can't sleep. If I had to bet, I would bet you like space movies, Mr. Sturdivant. You probably really like hobbits, too. You seem like the hobbit type.

In case you're wondering why I'm writing this letter (as I'm sure you are), I guess that means I've taken too long with The Greeting. I wanted to write to tell you about what really happened that night when everyone got real drunk at Andrew Turtle's house and then the incident that everyone knows about that got Tucker Brigley and Billy Pitt expelled and almost arrested too. Everybody knows about it because that's what everyone has been talking about in the hallways in between classes, in the library, in the cafeteria, all over school and on Facebook, Instagram, and Snapchat too. What do y'all teachers talk about during lunch anyway? I'm sure it's been a topic of discussion at some point for you. I'm sure y'all don't just talk about grading papers and tests and leftovers. I bet y'all gossip worse than us kids do.

Whenever I see Aunt Mildred appear in my room as an apparition (I remember that word from when we read *Macbeth*) she's always wearing the same thing: a red blouse, a pair of overalls, those beaded necklaces, jingly bracelets, and long, loopy-dangly earrings she always wore. Her earrings remind me of the dream catcher Daddy hung on the wall in the kitchen that he bought in Cherokee when we visited there one summer. The thing though that's always different about Aunt Mildred's ghost from when I remember her when she was alive and not a ghost, is she's always wearing big sunglasses now. They take up half of Aunt Mildred's face. She doesn't tell me why she's wearing them, but I'm sure she's covering where her husband Dirt hit her. Her husband's real name was Donald Dirt McGirt and he's just about how you imagine someone with that name would be. That's not how Aunt Mildred died, but when she comes to see me, she always says the same thing: "Don't ever let anyone treat you like you're lesser."

Everyone knew how Uncle Dirt beat on Aunt Mildred, but no one said anything about it. Even Daddy, who was also Aunt Mildred's brother. She started to hit him back, either with her fists or her sass, and just when Aunt Mildred clearly started getting stronger than Uncle Dirt, she got breast cancer, and that's how she died. I think she was mad at herself for wasting all that time on a man who wasn't any good for her. I was mad at God because why would he give Aunt Mildred cancer like that just when I needed her. I was thirteen. I believe in ghosts, but I'm not sure they come from God.

Before I get into The Body of this letter, the "Meat and Potatoes of what you want to write," as you say in class, how come you have so many cats at your house? I only know that because Sarah Braxton told me you sometimes ask her to feed your cats when you go out of town. I think I'm more curious about the cats than where you go when you go out of town. I asked Sarah how many cats you had, and she said, "I don't know, maybe five." Jeremy Russell would probably call that a gang of pussy or a pussy riot or something gross and inappropriate like that.

The truth is, I think, there are many ways to understand what really happened that night. For instance, when did the night really even start? Was it when the party at Andrew Turtle's house started? That was at about 9:30. I was sober the whole time, even though me and Sarah were both carrying bottles of Coca-Cola Zero mixed with rum (hers was actually mixed with rum, mine wasn't). I'd argue that, no, the night didn't start when the party at Andrew Turtle's house started.

Did it start earlier, then, maybe when it started to get dark, after our team, the Athens High Jaguars, beat the Cary Imps by one point at the buzzer when Tucker Brigley made a three-pointer and everybody ran onto the court and was jumping around and celebrating like it was New Years Eve (that is my sixth simile so far in this letter, so when you say I need to have more figurative language in my writing, is that what you mean?). Everyone was lit.

Here's what no one knows. At the beginning of the game, just before tip-off when all the players on the court shake hands and shake hands with the referee too, Tucker looked over at Billy, our class president, who was on the bleachers with the rest of us, the gym was packed, and they made their signature hand-signs to each other which everyone gawks at because they are best friends and basically run the school. I don't really care about it, and I guess it does look kind of cool, but I bet they've practiced it a million times which makes it actually not that cool but no one will tell them that anyway. It was how they looked at each other, like they thought they owned everything, that put fire ants in my britches.

Earlier that day in Psychology class, I sit next to Tucker and the teacher was going on and on about cognitive behavioral therapy, and Tucker had his laptop open like he was taking notes, but then Billy messaged him on Skype like: *Yo!*

I could see Tucker's screen light as day, so why wouldn't I look.

Yo, Tucker typed back.
Yo you think she'll say anything
Tucker wrote: *Sarah???*
Yeah
Bitch better not.
U sure?
Chill bro
U still got those pics tho?
Took them off my phone but I got them
Aight good
Later tonight at Turtle's
After the game?
Yep
Yep
Out
Out
One

Sarah's on the Gymnastics team. She's cute and short. I run Cross Country and have freckles and moles. Sarah's really cute. I'm lanky and have big earlobes. People say Sarah looks like Reese Witherspoon, which is to say, yeah, like, she's really cute. She's quiet though and a kind of sweet gullible that's dangerous. Maybe that doesn't come out in class, Mr. Sturdivant, but believe me, she's the worst kind of sweet gullible. If you were being silly and said you needed to borrow a dollar to buy something free, she wouldn't hesitate to give you a dollar or two. She's book smart, but when it comes to street smarts, she's about as useless as a crooked nail. But, like I said, she's really cute, and that's usually more important when you're a girl. At least in high school.

She had told me what happened. She tells me everything, even bad stuff, and then makes like it's nothing. She was over at my house and we were watching reruns of *How I Met Your Mother* and sort of out of nowhere she said, "Can two boys take the same girl to prom?"

I gave her a look. "What in the world are you talking about, Sarah?"

"I think Tucker and Billy are both going to ask me to prom, and I want to go with both of them."

"Sarah," I said, "they both got girlfriends. What makes you think they're going to ask you to prom?"

As you know, Mr. Sturdivant, Tucker goes with Melissa "Miss Everything" Evans whose Daddy is a preacher, and Billy goes with Jennifer Spivey, probably the best head cheerleader we've ever had.

Sarah said lately she'd been staying late after practice to get her balance beam routine down and she'd see Tucker in the lower gym, too, and he would come over sometimes and watch her and just, you know, as she said, chit chat and small talk. Her North Carolina accent is even thicker than mine, so when she says chit chat and small talk, she means he's being flirty. And, besides, no guys just small talk with girls wearing leotards.

Every weekend there's a house party somewhere and some parents are funny. For instance, Andrew Turtle's folks actually let Andrew have these parties. Mr. Turtle stays in his garage fixing whatever it is he fixes, maybe cars, and Mrs. Turtle sits right there at their kitchen table and smokes Doral Lights, one after another. She takes everybody's car keys at the door, and before they leave, she makes them blow into the air, like she's a breathalyzer, and even makes some walk in a straight line. "Ha," she'll say, "you ain't getting your keys. You can stay here if you need to and sober up." Like I said, some parents are funny. Mrs. Turtle looks crazier than a three-headed serpent sitting there telling off drunk high school kids about the dangers of drunk driving when she's the one who tells her son, yes, it's okay to have a house party when I'm at home sitting at the kitchen table watching reruns of *The Golden Girls*.

I mean, I guess she means well, like, she thinks it's safer when she knows where everybody is drinking since kids will get out and do it anyway. I understand that, but it's like she's condoning all that happens upstairs where the party is too. The stuff she doesn't know about.

Sarah told me it happened a few times. Once or twice in Tucker's black Escalade in the parking lot down at the lake where nobody goes after the sun goes down. Once or twice in The Yard at school. In the bathrooms in the basement by the Electronics workshop. There are no hallway cameras down there and the stalls are bigger in the bathroom because that's where they used to have to roll in the wheelchair kids before they made that big ramp at the front entrance of the school. Once or twice, late night, at Andrew Turtle's house, after midnight and closer to one or two when everyone was finally sleeping or passed out and Mrs. Turtle took all the leftover car keys to her bedroom to hide.

It started with Tucker in the lower gym and his small talk and then him taking her small hand in his big palms. He's almost six foot three. Tucker says something cute, and they kiss, and then there's always the walk to some place "more quieter," Sarah says. Sarah says it's always just them two, her and Tucker, and nobody else is around.

"You like that," Tucker says when he places his hands all over Sarah, like he's caressing her, but really he's just lying to her and he knows she's going to say *yes* on account of how dangerously gullible she is.

Here's the real Meat and Potatoes, Mr. Sturdivant:

After a while of Tucker heavy petting and kissing on Sarah, he gets her to do whatever he wants her to do, and

I won't go into detail about how powerful a boy like Tucker Brigley can be whilst he is with a vulnerable girl like Sarah Braxton. Some synonyms for vulnerable would be defenseless, exposed, liable, sensitive, susceptible, weak, unguarded, tender, sitting duck, and wide open. I know there are a lot of girls like Sarah Braxton.

I mean, part of me wants to think, it's difficult to blame them completely. I mean, I can see how some girls go blank and turn inside out. I mean, who wouldn't want to be the girl who hooked up with a boy like Tucker Brigley or Billy Pitts. Boys that will run the world one day, one way or another (Tucker's daddy is a judge; Billy's daddy is a doctor). But then Sarah told me about how Billy started showing up too and he started to touch her and they took pictures and filmed Sarah with their phones in all kinds of dirty porno-like ways and about how Tucker said the last thing Sarah would want would be to see that footage somewhere where everyone could see it, wouldn't that be awful. Sarah told me it wasn't a big deal, like she does everything, like nothing in the world is a big deal except for mastering her balance beam routine.

I told Sarah about Aunt Mildred. About how Uncle Dirt beat on her and all, but about how Aunt Mildred acted like it wasn't a big deal for a long time. And then I told her how she figured it all out when it was too late and her time on earth was limited, and then I told her about how she visits me and then I dropped the line to her.

"Sarah," I said to Sarah, "don't let them treat you like you're lesser."

"What do you mean?" Sarah said.

"They're taking advantage of you, girl, and they know better."

She said, "No, they're not, Amanda. They said they like me, like a lot a lot. And, I like them. Besides, I don't want to get anybody in trouble."

Sarah needed an intervention. Jeremy Russell would have said Sarah had "rats in the attic."

I knew what I had to do then.

I was going to give those boys exactly what they wanted.

The night started when I acted like I was drunk and Mrs. Turtle said she'd be happy to call my parents and talk to them about me staying. Are you crazy, I thought. My Daddy would have driven straight to the Turtle home and dragged me out of the house with one hand, whilst flipping Mrs. Turtle the bird with the other. I was already supposedly staying the night at Sarah's anyway, so it didn't matter. "I'll just crash on the couch upstairs like everybody else," I told Mrs. Turtle.

Sarah was really drunk. So was everybody. It was that type of night. That's what happens on buzzer-beater nights in high school. Everybody gets drunk. Most everyone was passed out in the big living room, but there were a few bedrooms upstairs too.

Mr. Sturdivant, you know what it looks like, I'm sure. Tucker and Billy stand about two feet apart. Their shoulders wide and stances sturdy and then they do their routine, which goes fast: they side five both palms and then the backs of their palms and then go pound, pound, pound, pound with their fists, then do something with their fingers that looks like "the itsy-bitsy spider," but it's way more macho, then they high five again but this time higher in the air, then they King Kong their chests two or three times, then they fake-box a few jabs at each other, then they bro-hug and yell, "One." It's all about as silly-looking as square dancing, if you ask me.

Too bad Tucker isn't as pertinacious with his phone code (*pertinacious* was the SAT word of the day the morning I took that God-awful test). When it was all quiet that night at Andrew Turtle's house except for the one TV on playing infomercials about Mane 'n Tail shampoo and the moonlight slivered through the blinds, I got up and tiptoed around upstairs, poking my head in each room, staring through darkness until I found Tucker and Billy and the rest of their highfalutin clique sprawled every which way on cushions and pillows and bed sheets. It was dark, but the moonlight creeping in made it so I could still see good enough. The Turtles live in one of the more-fancy Cary neighborhoods, which means everyone in the family can have at least two rooms to claim for his or herself. People only get into trouble with all of that space if you ask me. On the floor, Tucker was lying face up, snoring, and Melissa Evans was hugged up to his side in a way that her preacher Daddy wouldn't like. I knew Billy was somewhere in the room too, because I could smell him, which is to say I could smell his cologne, which I would call The Drunk Skunk if I could name it. That's what he smells like to me.

Tucker carries a little kiddy Elmo book bag to every party. It's another one of his things. Boys and their things and their ding-a-lings. That could be the title of a country western song, don't you think, Mr. Sturdivant? Tucker left his stupid Elmo bag by the door. I took it to the bathroom and realized this was all going to be much easier than I thought because his iPhone was right there in the front pocket. I had a few plans in mind, and Aunt Mildred approved of all of them. I punched the ID Sensor and guessed correctly on the first attempt with the passcode: 2388. 23 is Tucker's basketball number and 88 is his football jersey number. How's all this shaping up for Dramatic Irony? If I had to bet, Mr. Sturdivant, I'd say you know how this is all going to end.

I started taking pictures of myself with Tucker's iPhone. I mean the kind of photos that Sarah was telling me about. I knew that wasn't enough though, and Aunt Mildred gave me another idea. I started to text them to Billy with Tucker's phone.

Yo Billy check these bro u won't believe what I got this

bitch to do . . .
Just a little Rum and Coke and popped her the pills you got me . . .
Worked like a charm . . .
She was on my cock suckn n screamin for the venom
Then it was on
One . . .

I've been around boys long enough to know how they code switch and can turn into locker room talk quicker than striking lightning.

Then I texted me. The pictures first and then:
Remember these?
U r the one who said you wanted it
I know you wont try anything, right?
See you in Spanish chica ;)

I'm not too good in Spanish class, as evidenced by my C+ report card and Daddy who says, "I reckon a C+ means you're not too good in Spanish," but *No nos tratarás como una perra*, Tucker Brigley and Billy Pitts. We're not your bitch.

Now, do I know all what Tucker and Billy have to do with pills and whatnot? No, but that doesn't mean there might not be some truth in it. The real question is why does all this happen in the first place? I mean about boys and the things they do to girls? When I ask Aunt Mildred she doesn't say anything. I just hear her dream catcher earrings dangling in the dark. It'll be like that for a while, quiet except for all the unanswers circling around my bedroom and then Aunt Mildred will laugh like she does and that makes me forget for a minute about all the other things I'll have to take care of.

Mr. Sturdivant, those boys started it.

They'll be all right.

They'll survive.

They'll just go to another school, move, start over without flinching, and end up being safe from everything in the world like their daddies because they're rich.

I'm not sure about Sarah Braxton.

On the following Monday I was in my counselor's office, crying about how something bad happened over the weekend, but I wasn't sure I remembered it all clearly because of all the alcohol at the party. I showed her the pictures on my phone and then it all ended for Tucker Brigley and Billy Pitts. They confiscated their laptops and phones. There were other girls. I knew there would be. I'm sure you knew, too, Mr. Sturdivant. Everybody kind of knows, right. That's what's so thought-provoking and compelling about it all. How the world works and all and how everybody knows how it works.

A clever way to end this informal letter, Mr. Sturdivant, might be to jot down a quote from literature that sort of recaps all of the main points, but to be honest, I reckon I'm a little tired of clever and what people want.

I want to build a house one day whilst blasting Guns

N' Roses on some loud speakers.
How's that for an ending?

Respectfully,

Amanda

P.S.: I guess I am a little curious about where you go when you go out of town.

"FATHER LIKE LION"

When I came home from studying at a friend's house one night, Mom was in the kitchen cleaning up a mess that looked like a tornado made it. Her face was swollen, but she wasn't crying. She had a glass of gin near her. I ran straight to the garage, because I knew that's where Dad would be. He was always in the garage drinking and fixing stuff. I shoved him and told him to pick on someone his own size. I was in the tenth grade.

"Clayton," he said, "you don't want to start a fight you can't finish."

That's the best advice he ever gave me that he really meant and that line will stick with me forever. *Don't start a fight you can't finish.* Dad didn't take too nice to me shoving him like I did, so he flung himself at me. I was already taller—and much quicker—than him. I bear-hugged him and then swaddled him in a full nelson. I told him if he hit Mom like that again, I'd kill him. I held him tighter and thought about going ahead and doing it.

He said, "Mercy, son, mercy, I can't barely breathe."

I let him go.

He coughed like he had a sponge stuck in his throat and then begged me to forgive him.

I pointed at him and said, "Don't ever do that again. I mean it."

That night I thought I was invincible.

Before my son was born, my wife asked me what type of father I wanted to be. She was very pregnant. It was after church where we had been holding hands and praying together to a God I wasn't sure I believed in anymore. I thought about her question and then thought about sin. I thought, first, I want to be a father who doesn't get drunk. I want to be a father who doesn't watch porn, except for when the wife wants to, of course. I don't want to be a father who yells and screams at nothing. I don't want to be a father who does bad, even if everyone else is doing bad too. It's funny, I was thinking about fatherhood in the negative. All the things I didn't want. All the things I was convinced I saw in my own father.

It wasn't always like that.

When I was two or three, he'd scoop me up in his arms, cross one leg over the other, set me on the instep of his boot, and bounce me up and down like I was galloping on a horse.

"Hold on to the horsey," he'd say again and again, bouncing me so I laughed until my belly burned warm.

There were the fishing trips that I can still see in my mind like it was yesterday. I didn't like the messy worm-hooking. I liked just sitting there with Dad, being quiet on the bank of the lake. All the sounds and smells in the stillness. I liked it, too, when Dad took out the bucket of catfish feed and we threw out handfuls at a time and watched it sprinkle on the water. It was enough for me to just toss it out like that to the fish to eat for free.

My son doesn't look like me. I'm white. He's black. I've got blue eyes. He's got brown. I told my wife that more than anything I wanted to be a fair and honest father.

"You'll be more than that," she said.

Growing up, I only remember playing ball with Dad once in the cul-de-sac. I told him I wanted to shoot some hoops before practice.

"You can't just play ball all day," he'd said.

I was on the way out the door, the ball already spinning in my hands, but Mom told Dad to hush and put some shoes on. He put on his work boots. I only remember Dad always wearing work boots or dress shoes. Never anything else. We were in the father-son Indian Guides program and I remember one year our tribe took a trip to the coast to look for shark's teeth and to see the landmarks where the pilgrims and the Native Americans supposedly lived peacefully, for a time at least, and my friends and I laughed at Dad, even though he didn't see us, because he still wore his polished penny loafers out on the beach even though he was shirtless and in his swim trunks. My Indian name was Running Deer. I can't remember what Dad's name was.

I don't recall how old I was, but one day, Dad said my thumb-sucking had to stop. Every night from then on, before bed, he painted clear nail polish on my thumbs and told me only crybabies sucked their thumbs.

When I was in first grade, my best friend and I thought it'd be funny to make our own version of Ms. Buckley's song she'd recently taught us, which was "Old MacDonald Had a Farm." We sang about the female body and all its parts. I don't even know how we could've known those words then. That night, after Mom got off the phone with Ms. Buckley, Dad told me to lie across his lap and not squirm.

"If you do," he said, "you'll get more than what I plan on giving you."

He had a Ping-Pong paddle in one hand and lowered my trousers with his other, so my buttocks sat bare and naked in the air. I could hear Mom crying in the background, as I yelled to Dad that I was sorry and would never say bad words ever again.

When my son was finally born, I started to believe in God again. I didn't want to watch, but in the moments before he emerged into the world, the doctor propped a mirror in between my wife's legs. I was by her side, yelling *push,* and letting her squeeze my hand like it was a stress ball. I saw my son's head pass through the birth canal, and I couldn't help but wonder how impossible it all seemed. He was almost seven pounds.

After that night I put Dad in the full nelson, Mom and Dad split up for good a few months later. They had already been legally separated for a while, even though I didn't know. I always thought Dad was working—I knew him to be an accountant—but he was at the farm instead, living his other life, sleeping with his girlfriend named Michelle who was much younger than Mom. To Dad, the farm was acres and acres of resurrection and Jesus Christ. He thought he could just start over and be a new man there. A new Dad.

Once Mom and Dad's divorce was final, I didn't visit him until college, and Mom never pushed the issue with me either. Dad still visited me when I was in eleventh and twelfth grade. He'd drive down on weekends every once in a while. He even made a few weekday trips down to Raleigh just to watch me play ball, despite his thinking that the city was all a "rat race." I was on Varsity then, killing it, 3-pointer after 3-pointer.

I got an earring and Dad asked if I was a fag.

"A what?" I said.

It was a Sunday morning. We were at Waffle House eating breakfast. He was getting ready to drive back up to the farm, which was four hours northwest of Raleigh.

"A fag," he said. "Are you one of these?" He flopped

his wrist out into the air. "Are you tootie fruitie? A nancy boy? A fudge packer? Do you like men like that?"

I laughed at him, and I'll never forget the way he was looking at me. Like he was ready to say goodbye to me forever.

"Dad," I said, "faggots wear them in the other ear." I grabbed my right earlobe.

He shrugged his shoulders and took a sip of his steaming coffee. "Well, I didn't know," he said. "I was just making sure." He still looked at me hard like if he stared hard enough, he'd find something that would prove I wasn't once one of his sperms swimming around in Mom's uterus.

The thing is, Dad and I look just like each other, and I can't help that. I have his nose and his hair and the mole that sits on the far left side of my cheek that I have to shave every few days. When I was a senior in college, Mom called and said Dad was in the hospital. I hadn't heard her say "Dad" in a long time. She never asked me about him. We didn't have reason to talk about him. I didn't even think she had his phone number at the farm.

"He's been in an accident," she said.

Dad fell from the loft in the barn. I figured he was drunk—or had been drinking—but it was the floorboards that were loose. He stepped right through and fell more than fifteen feet directly on his back. He was lucky to be alive. At the hospital, everyone looked at me, like they were looking at a younger version of him. I could feel it.

Dad's girlfriend Michelle stepped out to get him something, which I took as code to give us time to talk. I felt sorry as hell for him lying there on the hospital bed and all those tubes were plugged in him.

"Well," he said, "I guess this is what you've been waiting for."

I rolled a metal stool by his bedside then and sat. "What do you mean?"

"You hate me," he said, "and I know it. Ever since—"

"I don't hate you, Dad," I said, even though I did. "You're just hurting. How do you feel?"

He laughed then. "How do you think I feel?"

Being with Dad made me think about everything bad I had ever done in my life. He was like a reminder, to me, of my own sinning. At that time, when I was drinking my way through school, I had been dating this girl named Kelli who I could easily guilt into having sex with me. It was easy, because *You know,* I'd say, lying hugged up with her like a pretzel in her bed or mine, *we've already gone so far, Kell, and, you're so wet, and having blue balls is real and hurts.* She always drank as much as I did and even more some nights. I'd keep kissing her until she'd say *okay* or fell asleep and then I'd just penetrate her anyway, with or without a condom, I didn't care. It was easy and I could get away with saying shit like *Let me just put it inside you for a little bit,* and then I'd just do it even if she didn't say yes, and then I'd laugh about it the next day and tell her I was drunk and so was she, but I knew I wasn't, and I convinced her it was all right. Better yet, I could convince her she was the one who wanted it more. I wondered what Dad said to guilt Mom and what all he made her do.

I visited Dad every weekend when he was laid up at the hospital. I didn't really have an excuse. My college was just an hour from the hospital where he'd been helicoptered in after the accident. I took Kelli a few times, and Dad spoke to her like he was a gentleman. One night, after we'd returned from seeing him, we were both real drunk, and she went on and on about how nice Dad was and how I looked just like him, and I shoved her into a wall and told her to shut the fuck up. She sat up against the wall and started laughing at me. I punched a hole in the wall then, right by her head, and before I stormed out of the apartment, said, "You stupid bitch."

My son is close to two now. I like to take him on walks. It doesn't matter where and, when it's just me and him on a walk in the neighborhood, I let him lead me. He'll walk a few steps, look back at me and smile, make some noise, like *da-da-da-da-da-da,* and maybe point to something around us, and then go back to walking. I do the only thing I can do, which is smile back and talk to him and bend down and kiss him on the forehead and follow him wherever he wants to go. I pick him up when he falls and distract him when he's going somewhere he shouldn't or can't yet.

After college, I had to leave. Mom understood, which is the toughest part for me now when I think about my parents. All that time and all my energy—all my anger and hate—were geared toward Dad, when I should have given my Mom more of me.

The day before I left for the Peace Corps, she drove me to REI and spent way too much money on a pair of hiking boots I absolutely did not need.

"You're going to Africa for two years," she said, "You need a good pair of boots."

She bought me a few other things too. A new backpack, clothes that were made of something synthetic and sweat-proof, energy bars, a Nalgene bottle. I called Dad the night before I left. He was back home at that point, moving slowly with his recovery. He was walking and all, but he'd have to take it easy for a long time. That meant farm work was out of the picture. He went back to consulting on finances and taxes. He told me he and Michelle were going to get married.

"Congratulations," I said.

"You'll probably have a brother or sister when you get back," he said. I felt even worse for him then, but I didn't say anything.

After the silence was too much for him, he said: "I love you, son. Be safe over there."

I said, "Good-bye, Dad," and hung up.

The boots were of no use, but I never told Mom that. I didn't realize the tropical savanna would be so sandy. I was picturing high green grasses waving in the African breeze, red clay soil and magnificent mahogany forests, lions and elephants. Instead, I got village foot paths of deep sand and weak soil that was barely fertile enough to feed the village year round. I lived on a homestead with a family that harvested millet and drank goat milk at every meal. My room on the homestead was a thatched hut. I was a teacher at a small village school, but a teacher of what I wasn't sure. I had never been a teacher, never taught anybody anything in my life. Every night I sat and watched the sun set.

The sun.

The son.

Is it any surprise it's a homonym? At dusk, I laughed at the sun drooping below the horizon.

The son.

Tate Mundjego, the father of my village homestead, reminded me of Dad. Stoic and hard. Unwavering and determined. One night, after the sun had already set, he came to my hut, knocked on the door, and said, "Clay, Clay, Clay." No one in the village had figured out how to say my name correctly, as I had not yet figured out how to ask for simple things from them or make simple conversation with them in their language. *Tate* Mundjego's voice was hurried and loud.

I went to the entrance of the hut, and there he was standing firm and tall. He held a sturdy piece of rubber that must have been ripped from an old tire.

"*Aeeno, Tate,*" I said, *Yes, father.* Mundjego was his last name.

Behind him, I noticed, was his son Pau. It was barely light out, but the sky was full of stars, and Pau's face was bloodied and swollen. I looked at *Tate* and said in English, without hesitation, "What's wrong with Pau. Why is he bleeding like that?" I talked with my hands and arms too, so he could tell I was in shock and meant whatever it was I was saying.

When I first met *Tate* Mundjego he'd told me he had been a freedom fighter. He said he was one of the first Sons of the Independence. He spoke German and Dutch and Afrikaans and a little English, on top of the seven or eight African dialects of his nation.

"He steal you. He steal you," he said there at my hut that night, and then he took my Sony Discman from his pants pocket. I hadn't even noticed it was gone. "I beat him for you."

I looked at Pau and then *Tate*. My heart sank then. Why had I brought a Sony Discman to a tiny African village anyway? So I could listen to songs of my past, close my eyes, and masturbate to all the girls I wished I could have sex with in my hut in the African wilderness? "It's okay," I said, which I quickly realized wasn't the right thing to say.

"Yes," *Tate* said. "Okay. I know, I know. You now. Your turn. You beat him *leegi leegi*." He handed me the Discman, then pushed the rubber whip toward me and stepped out of the way from Pau, gesturing for me to beat him. I didn't take the piece of rubber.

Pau just stood there, like he was waiting for it, expecting me to whip him, as his father had done to him. Pau stood there, helpless and still, waiting for me to take revenge. For me to take my rage and anger all out on him. He was silent, waiting. It was in that moment that I realized I did love my father. I had no choice, but to love him. He was my father. Despite it all, he was my father.

In high school, I used to steal shit from the mall. This was before everywhere had cameras and everything had sensor tags. Usually, I'd just steal clothing. My friends would make requests and even pay me, and then there I'd be, in some dressing room, layering my outfits with Tommy Hilfiger polo shirts and stuffing socks and fancy boxer shorts down my pants legs. The thing was, I didn't give a fuck, and I thought that was being a man. That was my mindset when I walked out of the stores. I was just like Johnny Depp in *Blow*, walking through the airport with a suitcase full of cocaine. I stopped all that one day when I watched a black man get wrestled down to the floor in a JCPenney. I don't know what he did, but I knew I was better than getting wrestled to the ground by a mall cop.

I didn't have the words to tell *Tate* Mundjego that he didn't need to beat Pau. I looked at Pau and said I was sorry. I repeated it, again and again, in English, "I'm so sorry, Pau. This wasn't supposed to happen. I shouldn't have even brought the stupid thing here." He just looked at me, like he didn't understand, like I was not one of him, but I was. I am too a son.

Tate Mundjego was confused. He was angry. He pumped his fists at Pau again, and Pau flinched, like his father was a starved lion. *Tate* looked at me, like I was weak, and I was.

I was nothing but weak and would be forever. He tried to make my hand take the rubber whip again, but I told him no. I apologized to *Tate* Mundjego. I said it again and again, "*Ombili, ombili, Tate gwandje,*" *I am sorry, my father.* I yelled it. I yelled it again to Pau, *Ombili, ombili,* my brother. I yelled it to the stars, "*Ombili, ombili, ombili,*" twinkling above in the forever African sky, until they left me there alone at my hut.

I am Running Deer. I don't know what demons Dad lives with, but I know mine. It was all a fight I couldn't finish then, and I never will. When it's just me and my son, walking in the neighborhood, when I pick him up, I kiss him hard and often, and I think maybe my black son will be gay and that will be the finest thing in the world, as long as he's fair and honest.

"WHEN THE COLOR STARTED"

Staring out the front window, BJ sees Mr. Jones walk across the yard to the porch, carrying a red clay pot of dried-out soil in one hand and his snotty-nosed bulldog Jericho in the other.

"Jeannie-June, Jeannie-June, Jeannie-June," Mr. Jones says, "you in there?"

BJ opens the big, wooden interior door and looks up at Mr. Jones through the metal screen door.

"Where's your Mama, Little Man?"

"In her room."

"What you doing?"

"Watching the bugs lightning in the sky."

"Do what?" Mr. Jones turns to the yard where the late summer dusk is settling and then he turns back to BJ. "Come on, Little Man, open the door. I'm about to get up out of here."

"Where you going, Mr. Jones?"

"Shit, I don't know, to the Motherland."

"The Motherland?"

"Africa. That's where everything comes from."

BJ looks at his arms and hands. "I came from Africa?"

"Yep. Mixed kids come from Africa too. Come on, Little Man, hurry up."

BJ unlocks and opens the metal screen door. BJ's mother always lets Mr. Jones in because he lives next door on the other side of the duplex. They live on East Lee, a small side street that runs parallel to Martin Luther King, Jr. Boulevard in downtown Raleigh.

"What you doing with that?" BJ says, pointing to the plant.

"Giving it to you."

"It looks dead."

"It ain't dead. Go and get your Mama."

BJ hustles to get his mother and when he returns, Jericho is breathing snot-bubbles on Mr. Jones' white Nike sneakers.

"Why's that dog in here," BJ's mother says.

"Can you take this plant, Jeannie-June?"

"It looks dead."

"That's what I said, Mama."

"Believe me, it ain't dead."

BJ watches his mother roll her eyes.

"Don't you want to take care of it, BJ?" Mr. Jones says.

"How do I do that?"

"First, put it in the basement."

"In the basement?"

"Yeah, it's warm enough in the winter and cool enough in the summer. Put it down there somewhere so the sun shines on it from the basement windows and give it a cup of water every other day."

BJ looks at the plant like it doesn't have a chance.

"This plant going to save y'all one day. Just wait."

"Where you going anyway?" BJ's mother says.

"He's going to Africa, Mama." BJ watches his mother poke her hip out.

"Do what—"

"I got to go, Jeannie-June."

"What are you talking about—"

"Little Man, you going to remember me?"

BJ nods yes. He doesn't want Mr. Jones to leave.

"Jeannie-June, you and BJ can take Jericho too, can't you?"

"What are we going to do with that dog?"

"Feed him. Play with him. He ain't going to pee in the house."

BJ hears his mother sigh, and before she says no, he says, "What's wrong with his tooth?"

"Oh, that. He just can't keep it in his mouth."

BJ thinks it makes Jericho's face a little crooked-looking.

"You want Jericho, don't you, Little Man?"

"Yeah, I guess."

"Jeannie-June, come on. Y'all got to take him for me."

BJ watches his mother and Mr. Jones stare at each other and he feels like he's in the middle of something. "Come on, Jericho," he says, leading him outside.

A few minutes later, BJ, who has cupped a lightning bug in his hands, watches Mr. Jones hurry to his side of the duplex. Jericho just stands in the yard and barks at the house. A car pulls in the driveway, but the windows are too tinted for BJ to see who's driving. Dusk is turning into night. BJ decides to let the bug go and after he does, he watches it float away.

Ten months later on a Saturday in June is BJ's eighth birthday. It's early in the morning and he's sitting at the kitchen counter eating a bowl of Honey Nut Cheerios. Jericho's lying on the floor. BJ's mother enters and prepares her morning coffee.

"Mama."

"What, son."

"You know the New River?"

She looks at him. "The new what?"

"The New River. It's the oldest river in the world. Mr. Stanley says that's ironical. What's that mean?"

She reaches for the pack of Doral Silvers on the windowsill behind the sink. She only smokes Dorals because they cost two dollars and ten cents at the vending machine outside the Big Lots, where the shopping carts sit. "It means," she says, taking one stick and turning to light it at the gas stove, "something like a surprise, I guess."

"Oh." The coffee machine gurgles and spits. BJ slurps milk from his bowl. "Did you know the sun is really a star that could blow out like a candle any second?"

She takes a long drag. "No, I didn't."

"Then the earth will get dark as night and colder than the freezer. I think that's what Mr. Stanley said."

"BJ, did you let Jericho out to pee yet?"

"No, Mama, not yet."

"Well, you better because you know—"

"I know, Mama, he's worth less than last month's coupons."

BJ swallows the rest of the mushy, sugar-covered cereal and skips to the front door. Jericho's collar tags jingle as he follows BJ. Outside, Jericho sniffs around the yard, pees on the back right tire of BJ's mother's grumpy old Honda Civic, and then barks at the house. BJ walks tippy-toed to the foot of the driveway to retrieve the paper and then he sprints back to the front porch.

"Jericho, come on," he says, holding the screen door open. "Mama's gonna squirt you if you keep barking at the house all the time."

In the living room, BJ turns on the television and plops down on the pea-green rug. He methodically lays out the newspaper and skims through each page and section. He reads some of the articles—the ones that look interesting—and paints pictures in his mind of each story. In the background, Wile E. Coyote is chasing the Road Runner, and every once in a while BJ looks at Jericho and says, "Meep Meep."

BJ's never held his real father, but he talks to him every month or so when he calls collect from prison. Only once did something happen that made BJ's mother wonder about it all. It was last year, when BJ was in first grade. His teacher Ms. Thompson called her on the phone after BJ had gone to bed.

"Is there something wrong?" Jeannie-June said.

"I don't want to startle you, Ms. Mooney, it's just, today, BJ asked something a little strange and I thought I should tell you about it."

Jeannie-June was smoking and moving about the kitchen, the long phone cord following her, coiling and curling. "He didn't say anything mean to anybody, did he?"

"No, no, no. BJ's a sweet boy. He always does his work, too."

"He better. That's how I raised him. What happened?"

"Well, in class today we were looking at photographs about past and present life in North Carolina—the country and the city life—and, well, BJ raised his hand and asked when did the color start."

"When did who do what?"

Ms. Thompson tee-heed and said she'd responded the

same way. "I just didn't understand what in the world BJ was talking about."

Jeannie-June pictured BJ sleeping in his bed, like he did, all balled up like he was going to cannonball into a swimming pool. "He didn't say anything to me about it today when he got home."

"Ms. Mooney, BJ just kept asking about the year color started and when I asked what he meant, he said the black-and-white photos must have come from a time when the world was only black and white and the color photos were from a more recent time like when the world finally got color and people started being different on the outside."

Jeannie-June took a drag of her cigarette. "Well?"

"I guess, I'm just wondering, Ms. Mooney, if maybe BJ is questioning—"

"BJ knows his Daddy is black," Jeannie-June said.

"I didn't mean it like that, I just meant, well, you know, we have all kinds of families here. Some kids even got two mothers and, you know, kids are just curious."

"Thank you, Ms. Thompson, I'll take care of it," and Jeannie-June hung up the phone.

BJ is still head-down, buried in the newspaper, when he hears his mother in the kitchen. "Mama," he says.

"What, BJ? I'm fixing your lunch for later."

"I think there's a cat under the house."

"Do what?"

"Jericho knows something we don't. Maybe there's a cat underneath the house."

"BJ, there ain't no cat under the house. We got the basement, remember?"

"Maybe the cat's hiding somewhere around the house then. Cats can dig, can't they, Mama?"

"Cats climb, BJ, but maybe Jericho does know something we don't." She sets two bologna, cheese, tomato, and mayonnaise sandwiches on a plate on the counter and covers it with a piece of Saran wrap. She walks to BJ and bends down to where he's sitting on the rug to rub his back. She's still in her faded, pink cotton nightgown that droops over her body like a weeping willow in the rain sags over a creek bed. "Anything good in the newspaper today?"

BJ likes it when his mother rubs his back. "Just a bunch of stories," he says.

"Happy birthday, BJ. You know I love you, don't you?"

"Yes, Mama, I know it."

She stands then. "I got to go into work today for a bit."

"I know."

"I'll be home by three."

"K."

"We'll eat ice cream later."

"K."

"What are the rules when I go to work?"

"Don't make a mess."

"And . . ."

"Don't open the door to anybody."

"And . . ."

"Don't spend too much time in the basement."

"And . . ."

"Don't watch too much TV."

"Good," she says and walks back down the hallway to her bedroom to get ready for her four-hour shift at Marshalls.

An hour later and BJ's mother has left. Dust particles dance through the floods of sunshine shooting through the front window. BJ goes to the kitchen, eats one of the sandwiches, and drinks a tall glass of milk in a few big gulps. He notices Jericho's food tray is empty.

"Dang, Jericho. No wonder you're looking at me funny. You're hungry!"

BJ fills the empty milk glass with water and walks down the steep stairs to the basement. He opens the big, ten-pound bag of dog food and digs out a scoop into Jericho's tray, and then pours the water from the milk glass over the soil of Mr. Jones's plant. BJ painted the pot an amalgamation of bright-colored splotches, lines, dots, and curlicues: yellow, purple, turquoise, pink, orange. The lone stem plant has grown into a sprawling bush with rich, green leaves that smell something like citrus. BJ calls it his artsy-fartsy plant after one day when his mother caught him making a mess with his paint in the basement and said, "BJ, don't get artsy-fartsy with all that."

Going back upstairs, BJ plays with his toys; he's got GI Joes and Legos and an Etch A Sketch. After he tires of the toys, he walks to the kitchen for more milk and eats the second sandwich. He hears thunder and notices clouds are forming outside, but he doesn't think it can rain on his birthday. He plops down in front of the television again and this time he watches reruns of *Double Dare* on Nickelodeon, where kids get soaked with slimy neon goo. He drifts into a dreamy, long sleep there on the pea-green rug, but then wakes when he hears a loud thud. He looks at Jericho, who is looking back at him, his snaggletooth hanging out of his mouth. BJ looks outside. It's rained a lot, but the clouds have disappeared and it's sunny again. He hears another thud and realizes something is happening in the basement.

BJ can't believe what he sees. The artsy-fartsy bush has grown taller, stretching to the roof of the basement, and fruit—all sorts of vibrant colors and shapes—dangles from its branches. BJ looks around the basement and then at Jericho. "Dang, Jericho, what in the . . . " He can't finish his sentence. His head is spinning faster than the spokes of a speeding bicycle and then he hears the phone ringing upstairs.

"BJ."

"Yes, Mama."

"What're you doing?"

"Nothing."

"You're not watching the television all day are you?"

"No, Mama."

"Did you eat your lunch?"

"Hmm-mmm."

"Drink your milk?"

"Yep."

"I'll be home in an hour or so."

"K."

"BJ."

"Yes, Mama?"

"You're not playing in the basement, are you?"

"Nope." BJ hears his mother say, "Be good, son, I love you," and as he hangs up the phone, he hears more thuds.

The fruit has flooded the basement floor. It's muggy instead of cool, and the fruit keeps forming—right before BJ's eyes—and falling faster than he can catch or count. "Jericho, what are we going to do? Mama's gonna be so mad."

BJ thinks about science class with Mr. Stanley and he's certain nothing ever grows that fast. Earlier in the year, Mr. Stanley showed the class how to grow lima beans out of a cup, but that took almost until Christmas. What would Mr. Stanley say about all this, BJ wonders.

Layers of fruit are piling and mounting and the basement smells sweeter than honey. Juice squirts everywhere. BJ hears a knock at the door and then the doorbell ringing, and he thinks it must be the police or the fire department.

Upstairs again, he peeks through the front window and on the porch a man and woman catch his curious, worried stare. He ducks and lies flat on the floor, like he's a soldier lying still in the middle of an ambush. He can hear the fruit still falling *thud*.

"Well hello there," BJ hears the man say.

"Is your mother home," the woman says then.

Jericho barks at the door.

"Shhhh," BJ says. He has no idea who the man and woman are or why they're knocking. BJ thinks though they look safe enough. The man is dressed sort of like Mr. Stanley, the woman sort of like Ms. Thompson. Maybe they're teachers, BJ thinks.

"Is everything all right in there?" the man says.

Jericho's still barking, and BJ decides to break one of his Mama's rules. He stands, steps to the door, and opens it. He looks out through the screen door window.

"He doesn't bite, does he?" the woman says.

"Who, him?" BJ gives Jericho a look. "He can't bite anybody. He just barks is all."

"Is your mother at home?"

"Who are you?"

The man reaches in his pants pocket and pulls out a card. "We're with the CPS," he says, lowering the card so

BJ can read it.

"What's Child Protection Services?"

"Well, son, we just make sure little boys like you are safe at home and not alone."

"I'm not alone," BJ says, and he begins to wonder if something bad has happened to his mother. "I'm here with Jericho."

"Right," the man says, "that's a cool-looking dog."

"You sure it won't bite," the woman says.

"I'm sure."

"Is Jeannie-June Mooney your mother?" the woman says.

"Yes."

"And she's not here right now, is she, BJ?"

"How do you know my name and my Mama's name?"

The man laughs. "It's okay, BJ, we're just checking in on you."

"Well, do you know where your mother is?" the woman says.

BJ thinks this is a trick question.

Jericho is still barking.

"Jericho," BJ says, giving him a quick, sharp look. "Don't make me squirt you."

Thud.

Thud.

Thud.

"What's all that noise?" the woman says.

BJ wishes he hadn't threatened Jericho like that. "It's nothing. My Mama said I'm not supposed to open the front door to nobody. She's at work."

"Does your mother leave you home alone when she goes to work?" the man says.

BJ tries not to think about his mother dying. "Sometimes. Is my Mama all right?"

"Sometimes? How often is sometimes?"

"Today's my birthday," BJ says and then he wishes he hadn't said that.

"Happy birthday," the woman says. "Too bad your mother isn't here with you."

"It's okay. She loves me a lot." BJ feels like they're going to take him somewhere far away.

"Well, BJ, how about we go get you some ice cream for your birthday. Me and Cheryl can spend a little time with you until your mother gets home."

"Where's Mama and who's Cheryl?"

"Oh, my," the man says, "Cheryl, where are our manners? BJ, this is Cheryl, and I'm Tom."

Thud.

Thud.

Thud.

BJ watches Cheryl and Tom peer into the house, trying to figure out what's making all the noise.

"I'm eight today," BJ says, "but I'm one of the oldest in my class."

Thud.

"Smartest, too." BJ can't stop thinking about how sad he'd be if he couldn't see his Mama anymore.

Thud.

Thud.

"I bet you are," Cheryl says.

Tom's phone rings then and he steps off the porch.

Thud.

Thud.

Thud.

Cheryl leans down to BJ. "Listen, BJ, I know you love your mother, but she can't leave you alone like this at the house."

BJ sees a police car pull in the driveway then.

"I'm okay, really—"

"Sometimes, BJ, little boys and girls don't always know what's best for them. Do you know where your father is, BJ?"

BJ knows his Daddy is in prison and will be forever, but he doesn't say anything.

Tom returns to the porch. A policeman gets out of the police car and easy-leans against it. BJ thinks something really bad must have happened because the policeman is too relaxed and looks like he's got secrets.

"Say, BJ," Tom says, "you want to take a ride in the police car? You can play with the radio and the twirling lights. It is your birthday."

"What about Jericho?" BJ wants to say, "Take me to my Mama," but he's afraid they'll say she's gone forever too.

"Well, I think we can take Jericho along. What do you think, Cheryl?"

Cheryl nods yes.

BJ doesn't care about playing with the radio and the sirens and police lights, and if his Mama is dead, he doesn't want to be alive either. He wishes Tom and Cheryl would tell the policeman to go away and he wishes they'd just tell him the truth about what's going on and he wishes he could go back to the basement and eat the fruit. It's all spinning and he can't decide what to do, but he remembers his mother crying one day about a boy in the neighborhood who was shot and killed and BJ remembers her telling him over and over and over again, almost like she was mad, "Son, you're always going to be black first, which means you always—always—have to do what the police say, do you hear me?" He wishes he could think of something smart to do and he wishes his mother never left on his birthday to go to work. He's afraid of it all, but doesn't know what to do, so he thinks it's best to do what Tom and Cheryl and the policeman say to do, that's what his mother would want him to do. He breathes and says, "Okay," and opens the metal screen door.

Jericho bolts outside.

Thud.

Thud.
Thud.
BJ starts to walk outside with Tom and Cheryl, but then he thinks about what Mr. Jones said about the plant saving his life. "Mr. Tom and Ms. Cheryl, can I go get something real quick?"

"Sure, BJ," Tom says, "we'll wait in the yard with Jericho."

The basement is a swamp of fruit. The artsy-fartsy bush looks like it's tired, like it's worn out from all that work. BJ finally plucks one that's Smurf blue and a little bigger than a ping pong ball. He takes a bite. It's syrupy and sweet and the juice squirts from his mouth and runs down his chin. The meat of the fruit is light and refreshing. BJ stretches the tail of his shirt so it becomes a basket and fills it with the fruit.

He has a tough time walking up the stairs of the basement and opening the metal screen door. Once he steps on the porch, he sees Tom and Cheryl and the policeman look at him, like he's from another land.

"Hey," BJ says, "y'all want to try some fruit?"

He walks to the center of the yard and he's holding his shirt like it's a sack and he pokes out his stomach so he can balance the weight of the fruit. Cheryl and Tom and the policeman meet BJ in the center of the yard.

"I've never seen fruit like that before," Cheryl says.

"Me neither," Tom says. "It's so colorful."

"Where'd you get all this fruit?"

BJ isn't sure what to say, but settles on: "Africa." He watches them look at his fruit belly, like it's the first time they've seen fruit. Jericho is sniffing and peeing on everything.

"Africa?" Tom says.

BJ nods yes and pokes his belly out even more for them to take the fruit.

Cheryl reaches first and takes an oval-shaped piece. It's harlequin-colored, and when she bites into it, juice shoots every which way. Tom jumps and yells, "Yikes," but the juice still sprays his teacher-pants. It's all intoxicating then. The policeman laughs. Tom and the policeman take the fruit to try too. BJ watches them eat and everything in the world changes. Cheryl laughs and says the fruit is "sweeter than a summer watermelon."

BJ watches his mother pull up then in her Honda and park by the curb. He's so happy to see his mother again, especially on his birthday. Jericho barks as Tom and Cheryl and the policeman can't get enough of the fruit. BJ's mother approaches them in the yard. In one hand she holds a gallon of Neapolitan ice cream.

"Ms. Mooney," Cheryl says.

"Lord, this fruit is so good," Tom says and belly-laughs like he's drunk. "Hey Jeannie-June."

BJ's mother suspiciously smiles at them.

The policeman grabs another piece of fruit from BJ's belly, says, "Criss-cross applesauce," and sits cross-legged on the grass.

"BJ," BJ's mother says, giving him a look.

Everything's a mess now, BJ thinks, but at least Mama is here.

"Where'd you get all this fruit, BJ?"

BJ shrugs. "From the artsy-fartsy bush, Mama."

She stares back and forth at BJ and the three adults prancing around, eating the fruit. Cheryl takes another piece of fruit and so does Tom. And then another and another and another. They dance and the fruit smears everything, and all the while they giggle, and Cheryl says every once in a while, "I have to go to Africa to get more of this fruit."

Everything's sticky and thick and new, like when the color started.

ACKNOWLEDGMENTS

Stories in this collection appeared in the following publications: "Fight Night" in *The Bangalore Review*; "W.W.K.D." in *The Shanghai Literary Review* and under the title "Sometime Long Ago" in *Lunch Ticket*; "Chosen" in *Stoneboat Literary Journal* and in *Eunoia Review*; "Normal Earl" in *Prism Review* and *Spittoon Magazine*; "Suburban White Girl Love Affair (Or Stubborn Love)" in *Flying South Anthology*; "A Night at Ovell's Casino" in *Spittoon Magazine*; "What's Heavy" in *Five on the Fifth* and in *The Drum*; "The Garbologist" in *MoonPark Review*; "Informal Letter Written by a Student to Her English Teacher Whilst Having Too Much Time Left Over in Gym 2 After Finishing the S.A.T. Way Too Early" in *Pithead Chapel*; "Father Like Lion" in *Menacing Hedge*; "When the Color Started" in *Reservoir*.

I would also like to thank: Siurong for believing in this work; Jo-Ann Mapson, Edward Allen, Carolyn Turgeon, Richard Chiappone, and David Stevenson for their wisdom and guidance; my dear friends Monique Cover Stenning, Alan Barstow, Simon Shieh, and Chris Herzberg for spending time with early drafts of this work; and finally, my wife who is my first and last reader, my muse, and my love.

ABOUT THE AUTHOR

BRADFORD PHILEN was born and raised in Raleigh, North Carolina. He holds an MFA from the University of Alaska in Anchorage, and currently writes and teaches high school English in the Philippines, where he lives with his wife, kids, and dog Bear. This is his third book. His full list of publications can be found at bradfordphilen.com.

OTHER WORKS BY BRADFORD PHILEN

Everything Is Insha'Allah
Autumn Falls

www.ingramcontent.com/pod-product-compliance
Lightning Source LLC
Chambersburg PA
CBHW030737110726
47900CB00008B/2341